A JINGLE
JANGLE SONG

'*A Jingle Jangle Song* brings into the light neglected modes of daily, queer, racialised experience, and commits to being wholly new and strange. It's a triumph and I'm so glad Lurid Editions has put it in our hands again.'

Noreen Masud, author of *A Flat Place*

'To read *A Jingle Jangle Song* is to discover a missing link in the tradition of the 20th century lesbian novel. It speaks back to *The Well of Loneliness* and to *The Price of Salt*, it speaks forward to the Jeanette Winterson of *Written on the Body*. At the same time, the world it creates in its spare, compressed way is uncannily contemporary — encompassing celebrity culture, gender fluidity, and the politics of body hair.'

Leigh Wilson, Publisher, Spiracle Audiobooks

'The heartrending is audible . . . this novella is at once urbane, tender and brutal. Queer desire painted in vivid strokes and furtive dashes through protests and parties of 1960s London. To be devoured whole in one sitting.'

Helen Palmer, author of *Pleasure Beach*

'A lesbian love story set against the rapacity of the music business.'

Jane Cholmeley, author of *A Bookshop of One's Own*

LURID EDITIONS

Bristol

First published by Chatto & Windus 1968
First published by Lurid Editions 2026

Text copyright © Mariana Villa-Gilbert
Introduction copyright © Christopher Adams 2026

Set in Baskerville
Typeset by Eva Megías
Printed and bound in Great Britain by
Short Run Press, Exeter

A CIP catalogue record for this book is available
from the British Library

ISBN: PB: 978-1-0686906-0-0; ebook: 978-1-0686906-1-7

A JINGLE
JANGLE SONG

MARIANA VILLA-GILBERT

Introduction

Christopher Adams

While preparing to carry out some research on lesbian, bisexual, and queer women novels of the mid-twentieth century, I came across a handful of works by the same author. The author's correspondence with her publisher was housed in an archive, but the archive required permission from the author's estate to access the material. My working assumption was that all of the authors I was interested in were now deceased, and I was used to tracking down nieces and nephews, friends, or literary agents who controlled the copyright to the author's work. But I could find no obituary records for this author. Perhaps she was still alive.

After some online searching, I discovered an entry into an old copy of *Who's Who* — complete with an address in Cornwall. More searching revealed a phone number. Like most people of my generation, I loathed making phone calls. Nevertheless: sacrifices must be made in the name of research. I dialled.

A thin, distant voice echoed down the line.

'Hello?'
'Is this Mariana Villa-Gilbert?'

A pause. Had the line gone dead — or was she thinking?

'This is she.'
'Did you write a novel titled *A Jingle Jangle Song*?'
'What's it to you?'
'May I send you an email? I'll explain everything.'
'I don't *do* the internet.'

A long pause.

'But you may send me a letter. By post.'

And so began my relationship, in what turned out to be the remaining three years of her life, with the remarkable and enigmatic writer Mariana Soledad Magdalena Villa-Gilbert.

Mariana — or Max as she was also known — was born in 1937 to Walter and Ada Villa-Gilbert. Mariana had a sister Gerda, two years her senior. The family lived in Croydon until early in the war, when air raids forced their hasty removal to the countryside around Exeter in Devon. Mariana's early life was lived in relative luxury: her father invented and manufactured parts crucial to wartime aircraft (Mariana herself had a life-long interest in aeroplanes), and the family experienced a higher standard of living despite wartime rationing. But in 1944, her father died suddenly — and the fall-out would haunt Mariana for the rest of her life.

Though Walter left his wife Ada a considerable sum, Ada suffered from alcoholism and bipolar disorder, and she spent lavishly. She remarried a Polish RAF officer, Marjan Gorączko, who was himself an alcoholic and in the early stages of tertiary syphilis. In 1947, the family moved to Gorączko's hometown in postwar communist Poland. On the journey, what cash that remained was lost when Ada's fur coat (into which she had sewn the money) was stolen. Mariana and her sister Gerda — only 10 and 12 — spent the next five years in a prolonged period of near starvation and acute neglect. Unable to attend the local school because they were English, they spent their days reading the two books they had brought with them and wandering the countryside, first around Myślenice and later Zakopane. Both as a coping mechanism but also a way to keep themselves entertained, they developed an elaborate system of play and fantasy they termed *gra* — the Polish word for 'game'. The recurring themes in Mariana's works— manipulation and control, transgressive sexualities, claustrophobic environments, isolated settings — all likely spring from this profoundly traumatic period.

In 1952, with Marjan hospitalised after a mental breakdown, the British Embassy intervened and arranged for Mariana and Gerda to return to England, where it was discovered that Mariana had contracted tuberculosis. She spent the next several months lying almost motionless in hospital before being sent to a convent school in Cold Ash, Berkshire. Despite the large gap in her schooling, Mariana was precocious and demonstrated a talent for art and literature. She decided to attend what became Central Saint Martins, studying sculpture under Elisabeth Frink. But upon graduation she decided to devote her life to writing.

In 1963 she came to the attention of literary agent and former publisher Herbert Van Thal, who placed the manuscript for her first novel *Mrs Galbraith's Air* in front of Norah Smallwood at the cutting-edge firm of Chatto & Windus, which published writers such as Iris Murdoch and Compton Mackenzie. A lunch at the Ivy with Smallwood and Cecil Day Lewis followed, during which Mariana was so frightened she could barely speak. Nevertheless, Chatto decided to publish the book, and *Mrs Galbraith's Air* — about an affair between an adolescent boy and an older woman — appeared to positive reviews. Mariana's style — influenced by her love of Virginia Woolf — was dense, sensual, and deeply absorbed in capturing sensation, moment to moment.

Off of the positive reviews (if not the financial reward: the sales were not strong), Smallwood offered Mariana an advance of £150 for her next novel plus an additional £100 on general account. The money allowed her to work on *My Love All Dressed In White* (1964). Like *Mrs Galbraith's Air*, *My Love All Dressed in White* concerned a relationship between a beautiful adolescent and an older woman (his stepmother). Set in a crumbling country house, the novel developed a more haunting and queer atmosphere, signalling a turn toward ghostly subjects that Mariana would pursue in her short fiction. Another novel, *Mrs Cantello* — about an ageing bisexual novelist — appeared in 1966.

Mariana likely started composing *A Jingle Jangle Song* in late 1965 or early 1966. Her agent passed it to Smallwood in September 1966. By this time, Mariana had lost her publishers some £118: sales of her first three novels failed to cover their advances. Nevertheless, Smallwood — who throughout her career made long-term investments in writers — believed that Mariana was a true talent. *A Jingle Jangle Song* was a creative departure from Mariana's earlier works. While her previous novels had an ethereal quality about them, aided by their isolated or rural settings, *A Jingle Jangle Song* is set in the bustle of contemporary mid-1960s London. Mariana, who was now working in the music department of a WHSmith after the money on account from Chatto & Windus ran out, chose to explore the world of celebrity, pop-folk music, and counterculture. It was also her first novel to explore in depth an explicitly queer relationship between two women: folk singer Sarah Kumar and her older lover Mrs Jane Stankovich. In so doing, she became one of a handful of novelists participating in the creation of the queer women novel in Britain.

The first draft of *A Jingle Jangle Song* caused concern. The publishers felt that the Sarah Kumar was modelled far too closely on singer and activist Joan Baez, and they feared a libel suit. Mariana claimed she knew almost nothing about Baez and had not intended for a comparison to be drawn. (I am inclined to believe her, given that Mariana was living a reclusive life in Canterbury when she was writing the story — and that a closer comparison would be a female Bob Dylan.) Over the next six months, Mariana rewrote the novel, changing details about Sarah Kumar's backstory and identity. She even

— at the request of Chatto's lawyer — added a positive reference to Joan Baez by name, so that there could be no confusion. These patterns of changes to avoid libel suits were common in mid-century editing and revision stages, but there seemed an especially heightened concern when the text involved a queer storyline: to imply that a living person was anything other than heterosexual was both reputationally and legally dangerous.

After much back and forth, *A Jingle Jangle Song* finally had printing proofs prepared in October 1967. Artist Carol Barker, who had designed the dust-jacket for *Mrs Galbraith's Air*, was again commissioned for the dust-jacket, creating a striking image of a woman holding a pink guitar. The novel was published in March 1968.

Reviews were mixed. A glowing notice by Rivers Scott in the *Sunday Telegraph* refers to Mariana as 'a stylist of no mean cunning'. Though the folk-singer party world and relationship between Sarah and Mrs Stankovich had the potential to be 'sordid', the novel avoided becoming so because of 'Miss Villa-Gilbert's understanding of her main character and...the intelligence and sympathy with which she marries and counterpoints the strangeness of that character and (in the girl's eyes) of London itself'. The review concludes that *A Jingle Jangle Song* is 'A most vivid and perceptive book'. David Holloway in the *Daily Telegraph* also singled out the book for praise: 'Miss Villa-Gilbert is an utterly unexpected writer; the last book [*Mrs Cantello*] was gentle and withdrawn, this is tough and at times rather strident. The London scene is well observed and the attitude properly disenchanted'.

But the relationship between Sarah and Jane was subjected to considerable homophobic attack from

— inevitably — male reviewers. As a representative example, in a review titled 'A Man's World', Vernon Scannell opens with: '*A Jingle Jangle Song* is written by a woman and is mainly about women but it is a long way from being a lady's novel'. One of his chief complaints is that Mrs Stankovich's husband Anthony 'is the only male character in the book who is presented in any depth' but 'it is a measure of the novel's fundamental misanthropy that he is shown as pale, wet, and crudely insensitive to the rare quality of his wife's love for Sarah'. He continues: 'For non-lesbians like myself, the love scenes have a certain didactic interest but I found Sarah a lot less fascinating than both Jane and the author seem to find her'. It's noteworthy that Scannell's review appeared in the *New Statesman* — a progressive paper that had pushed for the decriminalisation of male homosexuality but that was, according to historian Elizabeth Wilson, also a paper 'where the oppression of women never rated a word'.

One other review in the British press stands out, by way of highlighting the bind in which *A Jingle Jangle Song* — as a pioneering novel about queer women — found itself. Irish journalist and feminist Mary Kenny, writing in the *Evening Standard*, called the book 'yet another stab at the definitive lesbian novel'. For queer novels of the mid-century, this, too, was a common line — not always of attack (though it could be employed as such) — but of assumption: that queer novels had a limited market, appealed only to a tiny minority group, and consequently more than a handful of them were unnecessary. There was not yet a sense that queer experiences could not be

- Elizabeth Wilson, *Only Halfway to Paradise: Women in Postwar Britain: 1945-1968* (London: Tavistock, 1980), p. 104.

summed up in any 'definitive' or single way: queer life requires — demands — a constellation of viewpoints. Kenny further called out *A Jingle Jangle Song* for criticism because of its somewhat demure approach to the physical relationship between Sarah and Jane: 'Come, come, Miss Villa-Gilbert; we did better in the dorm at convent school'. The critique is accurate — up to a point. Kenny seems not to consider how radical it was to have *any* literary material featuring queer women published at all — and by a pioneering literary publisher no less.

Indeed, since 1928, when the trial of Radclyffe Hall's *The Well of Loneliness* declared that literary depictions of relationships between women were inherently obscene (even while in real life they remained legal), a chill had settled over representation of queer women in British novels. Where queer women were represented, they were done so in more coded forms, or in the pages of genre fiction, such as in Mary Renault's 'hospital romance' *Purposes of Love* (1939), Nancy Spain's murder mystery *Poison for Teacher* (1949), and Dorothy Bussy's boarding school novel *Olivia* (1949). As the 1940s gave way to the 1950s, lesbian pulp fiction emerged as a popular genre — but only in American markets. The specifics of customs and obscenity legislation meant that these books could not be imported into Britain in large quantities. With a notable exception or two — e.g. Brigid Brophy's *The King of A Rainy Country* (1957) — novels that centred the lives and concerns of queer women in 1950s Britain remained shockingly scarce.

The situation began to change with the advent of the 1960s. In addition to the passage of the Obscene Publications Act (1959), which permitted authors to defend their work on the grounds of literary merit, literary writing generally became more open to presenting the intimate lives of women, their bodies, and their desires. For queer women's writing, the early and mid-1960s was a watershed moment, with the publication of titles such as Rosemary Manning's *The Chinese Garden* (1962), Maureen Duffy's autobiographical *That's How It Was* (1962), May Sarton's *Mrs Stevens Hears the Mermaids Singing* (1965), and Duffy's landmark experimental novel *The Microcosm* (1966). The decade also witnessed the arrival of the first British lesbian periodical, *Arena Three*, in 1963. But it is important to emphasise that queer women's writing remained on the very fringes of literary consciousness. Or to understand the scale a different way, consider this: from 1946 to 1967, around 49,000 works of fiction were published in Britain. Of these, around 166 titles featured a lesbian, bisexual, or queer woman character (however coded). If we focus on titles that actually had a substantial amount of queer representation, or that centred the experience of their queer woman protagonist, the total number of titles falls to about 30. That's 30 novels out of 49,000 over a period of 21 years. *A Jingle Jangle Song* is one of those 30 or so novels. With its composition and publication, Mariana was not only contributing to — but was in fact creating — the modern British queer women's novel. If the sexual relationship between Sarah and Jane is more erotic than explicit, this says more about mid-century conditions — what was and was not possible to write and publish when one had very few models to follow — rather than any prudishness on Mariana's part.

But between the accusation that *A Jingle Jangle Song* was too much 'about women' on the one hand, and 'yet another stab at the definitive lesbian novel' that didn't go far enough on the other, there was another voice that argued that the novel was important, refreshing, and connected with queer women readers. In the September 1968 issue of the influential lesbian magazine *The Ladder*, editor Barbara Grier (using her pen name Gene Damon) writes in her book review column on 'Lesbiana':

> For me the reward for searching through endless hundreds of books each year is the occasional title that makes all the boredom and all of the irritation engendered by many of them, worth it. The unlikely title, A JINGLE JANGLE SONG...is one of the special books.

Grier, who had a commanding knowledge of books featuring queer women characters, praises the novel for being 'compelling and, at times, intensely vital'. She also notes that the relationship between Sarah and Jane is 'very erotic but very well handled'. In her bibliography *The Lesbian in Literature* (1981), she gives the novel an 'A***' rating — her highest mark. The 'A' indicates the novel has a queer woman as its protagonist (as opposed to 'B' or 'C' ratings, where queer women might appear as minor characters); the three * indicate that the quality of that depiction is of the highest order. With such a rave review in *The Ladder* — whose readership was international — Grier was able to establish and promote *A Jingle Jangle Song* as the pioneering and important work that it is.

I have throughout this brief introduction tried to highlight *A Jingle Jangle Song*'s status as a queer text. But there are other points of entry into the novel, and other reasons it should be celebrated. It offers a vivid glimpse of 1960s music culture. Its biracial, multicultural protagonist seems freshly attuned to what feel strikingly modern concerns around questions of identity. The novel's structure and tone are reflective of experimental writing, particularly in mid-century feminist texts. Through the writing of the novel, Mariana herself was developing her own style, influenced by other writers such as Virginia Woolf, Brigid Brophy, Maureen Duffy, Katherine Mansfield, and Stevie Smith, marked by half-sentences, sudden turns and leaps. The first sentence: 'To the flat in Knightsbridge, overlooking the square' — shows a boldness, landing us in the middle of a journey. The novel is, for me, Mariana's most engrossing, the heady marriage of her prose and sensitivity to the world along with a milieu and propulsive plot that gives the novel an irresistible strength.

Mariana went on to publish two further novels — *The Others* (1970) and *Manuela: A Modern Myth* (1972), and later a collection of short stories titled *The Sun in Horus* (1986). But conditions at home were strained, overseen by the constant presence of her mother. Mariana, for instance, dedicated *Mrs Cantello* to Ada — but when Ada learned of this, she was furious. She seemed both resentful that Mariana should write anything publicly and also that Mariana had achieved some level of success outside of her sphere of influence. Mariana's job at WHSmith, which paid her one-third of what her male colleagues earned, and where she worked for some forty years, hardly left her with enough money to have much of life outside the family home. She, her sister, her mother (and for a time her mother's fourth husband) lived together in Canterbury until Ada's death in 1993. A few years later, Mariana and Gerda moved to Cornwall. Gerda died suddenly in 2004; Mariana survived her, living in the quiet village of Stithians until she died in her sleep in May 2023.

Mariana truly understood writing not as a commercial enterprise or a hobby but as an artistic vocation — a spiritual calling. I first knew of her work only through the six novels and short story collection that had been published during her lifetime. But after her death, she left me her copyright as well as the entirety of her unpublished material. When I collected it, the material filled four suitcases. Among the papers were numerous short stories, a play, at least eight novels, two autobiographies, and multiple poetry collections, including a moving collection written in the two years after Gerda's sudden death. Common themes include the environment, the natural world, pagan and feminist representations of divine womanhood, intimate relationships between women, gender identity — and cats. She was also an excellent writer of short horror fiction. The overall impression is of a person who, despite being almost totally ignored by publishers (there are many rejection letters among her papers), continued to write — perhaps out of instinct or habit, but also out of a deep sense of herself as an artist.

At an early point in *A Jingle Jangle Song*, Sarah Kumar catches sight of herself in a wardrobe mirror. She thinks to herself: 'She'd an idea she gave the impression she was fragile, which she wasn't' — an apt statement for a character in the novel who others try to cajole or pressure, but who ultimately pursues her own path. But also, I think, a fitting statement for the novel as a whole. For *A Jingle Jangle Song*, though it appears short and slight, is in fact a pioneering work of queer women's fiction, at the forefront of a (very) small clutch of novels that created the genre in Britain. And a novel forged out of the difficult personal circumstances of a writer who appeared fragile: but wasn't.

JANE

To the flat in Knightsbridge, overlooking the square. Their good friend John Graffman: op art, great wheels of colour that exploded at one out of the walls of his West One gallery. (Here, the cab turned off into Sloane Street.) She hadn't really wanted to come, didn't feel she was going to enjoy herself. Always such a mixed crowd at John's.

But then, getting out of the taxi, the limes in the square. No leaves yet, but evocative. (But of what?) And the evening warm, shadowless. Not a whisper. Oh yes: a bird in the square. The birds would be building soon, or had begun already.

Waiting, she saw her elongated self in the back bumper of a silver-grey sports saloon parked outside the house. (Someone had left a pair of shoes in the luggage space at the back.) There were other cars: she counted them for something to do. But Anthony had paid off the taxi, and together they went up the steps. Dreadful browns and reds and greys here in Knightsbridge, and all rather neglected looking. But she liked it: she always liked coming here.

In the bare, badly-lit hall - one distant chandelier, thick red carpet on the stairs, dark paint and gilt beading - she said:

'Not late are we? The whole thing seems well under way.'

Upstairs, the music thumped merrily. (He'd stereo, and all the rest. A bachelor, he could afford these luxuries.) No, Anthony said, he wouldn't have thought so. A few minutes perhaps, no more.

John - tall, dapper, with those little brown curls on the nape of his neck and a dimpled smile - met them on the second-floor landing. Instantly, though not because of him, she was glad she had come.

'Ah, there you are. I was beginning to think you mightn't come. Dreadful racket I'm afraid - can you put up with it? I've got Jake Gould here: do you know him? Gould Enterprises, a whole empire: pop promotion, that kind of thing. He's behind The What's Their Names, thinks they're going to be as big as the Stones. I do want you to meet him: he's quite a character. Terrific rumpus though: I'll be all complaints tomorrow.'

He'd had the flat done up when he moved in just before Christmas. Very clever and exciting. Splashes of bold colour, and plenty of mirrors, and some good paintings. One wouldn't have thought one was in the same old building one saw from outside.

There on the right, the bedroom door stood ajar. A small, narrow room. And, on the chest, the Queen Anne looking-glass he'd picked up at a junk sale and painted white. A ladderback chair had had the same treatment, was cushioned in mango to match the bedspread and curtains. But mostly white: the wardrobe too. The wardrobe had a long glass: confusing new dimensions, a sudden reversal of all she'd glimpsed at first. A whole crowd of young people sitting about on the floor, or lounging against the wall. Frail young men with limp hair: roly-poly girls, badly dressed. The usual crowd:

desperately if expensively unfashionable. But the ghastly thump thump had stopped and a girl had got up on the bed, was picking at a guitar. She had on a brief shift affair, seemed barely dressed. Flowered cotton: bronzy, and yellow, and flecks of red. Very slim. Brown legs. (And suddenly she remembered Greece, the Islands.) She thought she knew the face, but where? The television perhaps? Yes, that was it. But months ago.

She was singing something about Queen Jane - which Queen Jane she didn't know, only that the name was her own and she hadn't expected to hear it just then - and smiled in a rather secret sort of way, her head bent.

'Jane?'

She didn't answer immediately.

'Jane?'

'Here.'

'Do come along and meet Jake.' He took hold of her arm, moved her on into the sitting-room. 'Incidentally, he's terribly keen on Tony's work.'

She knew of him, certainly: something she'd read in one of the glossies. A pimply-faced, very young man in a Carnaby Street suit who'd made a fortune out of long haired nihilists like The What's Their Names. No more real in the flesh: little eyes, close set and shrewd, and enormous jewelled cuff-links. He turned from the stereogram, gave her the once over. She shook hands with him. His accent was neither English nor American: mid Atlantic, she supposed. He talked very fast, but didn't seem aware of her at all. They exchanged pleasantries of a sort. Next she knew, he'd got on to Vietnam. When, he wanted to know, and quite out of the blue, were they going to stop the fighting in Vietnam?

'Vietnam?' (Couldn't think what to say momentarily.)

'Yes, one does wish there was something one could do.'

He helped himself to a cigar, asked had she heard that McGuire disc Eve of Destruction? Great stuff, great. He struck a match, sucked aggressively at the flame. And then, after scrutinising her again, on to Anthony's sculpture show: he'd seen it, he went yesterday. It was great, great. What a gas.

'Yes,' she said.

But here was John again, with drinks.

'I was just saying about Tony's show: great.'

'Looks rather good, doesn't it? The gallery is right for sculpture shows of course: masses of space. But if I'd known you were interested dear fellow you could have had a ticket for the private view.'

'Oh, not to worry. Another time.'

'Ideally though sculpture should be shown in the open. Like that thing of Moore's you know - King and Queen. Up on a hill somewhere.'

'Oh great, great,' Gould agreed. But rather more interested in the general curiosity he aroused. He excused himself suddenly, went off into the crowd. A woman with enormous earrings.

And chatter, chatter, chatter. Gossip, politics, art. And new faces all the time - people were still coming. She didn't know any of them, never did, was sure John didn't know them all. Across the room, Anthony was lumbered with a dreadful bore of an old boy - an ex Academician who specialised in naughty water colours or some such absurdity. She admired him briefly (she was nowhere near as tolerant), but here was an extraordinary gentleman with shoulder-length red hair - was it a wig? - and what looked like a nineteenth-century coat in wine-coloured gaberdine. Fussy shirt too: all very, very. She couldn't think where he'd come from, hadn't seen him till now. But ridiculously wrong here: rather as though he'd dropped in on them, literally, from goodness knows where. Compere on a TV disc show, she was given to understand. He joggled his shoulders and did odd things with his neck while he talked, and it was Jake this and Jake that all the time. She didn't catch much else: the stereogram had taken over again. Everyone fairly screamed above it. (A kind of music she disliked intensely: middle minded, smooth, and with a copulatory beat.) It didn't matter anyway. Someone, going out, had left the door open. And on the landing was the girl with the guitar, but without the guitar this time. She'd the look, standing there, of a strong-featured young Spanish aristocrat. (But not Spanish, no. More Oriental.) Sallow, rather coarse complexion, and a high-bridged nose. The brows very fine, very dark, the mouth rather full. She smiled often, as though it were a relief.

She watched a moment, curious.

'John, who's that girl?'

'Which one? Where?'

Foggy, like the atmosphere. It annoyed her that she must explain, must point out. She didn't want to advertise her curiosity.

'On the landing.'

'My dear, didn't I tell you? Jake brought her along - I begged him. Frankly though, I didn't expect I'd get her. She flew in only this morning, left a reception to come on here. Her recording company: a small, private party. No press, because she's unofficial for a day or two

- hasn't arrived yet I mean. Very obliging of her though. I had to promise there wouldn't be any fuss of course, no letting the cat out of the bag and so on - Jake rang me before they came on here, made me vow. So keep mum, won't you dear? - Sarah Kumar. Striking though, isn't she?'

But her interest had cooled, snapped back on itself like a spring. She didn't know why. That she'd had to ask perhaps, had to make her curiosity public? And the way he babbled on like an excited schoolboy, quite raved. He'd all her records, he said, was quite a fan.

'No honestly, there's no one like her. She doesn't have an act in the accepted sense: no gimmicks, do you see? It's all personality. On stage she wears one of these shift things all in black and totes a black guitar, but she doesn't do anything - just stands there.'

'And sings presumably?'

'Oh yes, like an angel.'

'She doesn't look well. Is she drunk?'

He glanced quickly at her, then back at the girl. He said nothing momentarily, seemed astonished.

'I don't know: I hadn't thought. But let me introduce you to Sammy. Sammy S. Silver. I don't know what the S stands for - Silver perhaps? Samuel Silver Silver. Or Solid Silver. His real name's Froy. He blew in with Jake and the girl: never set eyes on him before.'

'Actually, we've already met.'

'Well, again. What did you make of Jake? He's rather fun really. I've got to know an awful lot of odd characters through him.'

'I'll try anything once.'

'Honestly though,' drawing her through the crowd with him, 'they're not all morons. Some are. But a fair proportion have been to university or art school or something of the sort. Jake's one of these self-made so-and-so's, but a good fellow all the same. Made himself a packet already.'

'Really?'

She didn't, after all, get near the disc jockey gentleman. He was signing autographs, generally exhibiting himself, and she began to feel she was a bit old for this sort of thing anyway. Not exactly aged, but well over forty and really not terribly interested in Sammy S. Silver. And the room, the atmosphere, seemed to have changed somehow: she was bored to death. She'd go instead to powder her nose.

But the girl had gone. A slight sensation of let down, of disappointment.

SARAH

They asked her would she sing for them again, these so un-hip hippies, but they had it all wrong. When she sang they looked like they'd got stomach pains or something, and she didn't see it that way at all. So this time she'd do something funny, make them laugh. A send up maybe. Yeah.

A nice, a real folk star smile for them.

'You remember earlier I sang you a Bob Dylan song? Okay, try guess who this is.'

She didn't have a mouth organ, but never mind. Also, her hair was too long. But she messed it up a bit first and, using a strong nasal tone, scratched an accompaniment on the guitar. Everybody relaxed, began to dig it at last. (Always she had this difficulty with English audiences.)

But it was all falling about somehow - those faces down there, everything. It all swung, glared. She felt hot, then cold. That white light just over her head burned behind her eyes, and the palms of her hands, her upper lip, sweated a little and it was like her head had floated off somewhere. She'd thought she was all right, but suddenly she wasn't all right. She'd drunk too much, was stoned out her mind, and had to get out of this place quickly. Everything in the room - the floor, the bed, the chair, the walls - was moving in on her with the nausea. Like seashore waves. Like she stood on the beach with her toes in the water, and the infinite dizzying expanse of the ocean rolling before her and each washing surge stronger than the last. Those kids down there were killing themselves with laughter, loved every minute. But then were struck dumb, goggled stupidly when she dropped everything suddenly, groped for the door. She knocked against something but didn't feel it: everything was soft, impalpable, swam away from her. She kept saying sorry but I out of here and they all fell back like she'd got the plague.

On the landing she caught hold of the banister, leaned over. Someone came. A face: she didn't know who. The face asked was she all right? She said she wanted the lavatory. But didn't know her own voice. It came from a long way off.

Now she opened a door, shut it carefully after her like she was making ready for a ceremony. All very deliberate, her actions. And only vaguely aware of the nausea, the moisture over her upper lip. A rush of cold air: an uncovered bulb somewhere, the light very bright. And everything clinically clean. A handbasin with bright taps: a big rectangular glass over the basin. The floor threw her about, like on a boat. She set her palm against the cold tiles on the wall. She could feel the cold, knew there was a surface, but like her hand wasn't her own and the wall was pulling away from her, falling back. Falling back, but taking her with it. Going somewhere together: a never-ending plunge into nothing. Turning slowly, the wall and herself, in space.

She hung over the basin for what seemed an age. Her hair hanging too but she couldn't be bothered, it just didn't matter. And sweated hot and cold and later, how long she didn't know, vomited a thin brown fluid. She saw it running away, and then the waste all bright chrome again but small pieces on the sides of the bowl. Another wait and then something more substantial. (Something she'd eaten at the other place. She didn't remember what.)

She missed the basin the second time, but that didn't matter either. She felt so bad nothing mattered.

And then came a draught of air again, and someone had hold of her arm and was saying it's all right now, and it was.

But a long way away.

SARAH

She woke damp and hot and she was lying on the bed with the mango cover. Under her, her clothes stuck to her body. Her mouth was open and the warm saliva ran from her lips, crept along her jaw and on into her hair. The light dazzled, so she shut her eyes again. It was very quiet at first: she couldn't hear anything. And then

9

she heard people going down the stairs and calling out.
And then, before she opened her eyes even, she knew
someone was in the room with her. Her mind began to
race: a man or a woman? (That was what Frankie did,
took advantage of her.) No, a woman. The face belonged,
she thought, to someone she knew. But then, funnily,
realised it didn't. She'd never seen her before. She knew
the room though, and all the things in it. But like it had
happened years ago, years and years. She didn't know
what the time was. Only that, if it was next day already,
she'd an engagement at eleven-thirty. She'd that spot
to record for a TV show they were putting on after
she went back. An articulate, discerning, sophisticated
woman. (Somehow she knew all these things at once.)
Wrapped in something dark with a lot of fur, like she was
cold. Like someone waiting at a railway station. Heavily
but beautifully made up, the eyes especially. The face
Italianate, renaissance. The make up maybe? Because,
in spite of the Anna Karenina eyes, distinctly English.
A typical English person. That nebulous quality: like
something seen through water. The features regular,
balanced, timeless, ageless: it was a bit like looking at a
painting. One of those cool English painters - oh, who?
She couldn't think. But seeing her there gave her the
same sense of time suddenly crystallised, frozen before it
could fall, she got from looking at old pictures. She ought
to say something, to thank her perhaps? But was terribly
embarrassed suddenly, didn't know how to begin. As it
turned out she didn't have to say anything: the woman
saw she'd woken, smiled at her.

'Better?'

'Thank you. I guess so.' She didn't know really.

All she knew was her head ached something sick and it had got tender in the pit of her stomach she wanted to go somewhere so badly. She looked at the ceiling a minute, then away again because the light hurt so. 'Do you have any idea what time it is please?'

A pause while she looked at her watch. 'Nearly ten past six.'

She couldn't think a moment.

'Six? Six what?' And then, because maybe it had sounded rude: 'I beg your pardon?'

'Six o'clock in the morning. You've been asleep nearly seven hours.'

She screwed her eyes up tight.

'Ye Gods, I'll have to leave this place wherever it is. I got all kinds of things to do.'

'I'd rest a few moments if I were you.' The woman got up, went to the chest and opened her handbag. 'I've some aspirins here. I'll get you a glass of water. You stay where you are.'

She was glad to stay where she was, everything ached so. Her head, her stomach. And her limbs all stiff and cramped.

'What happened to the party?' she asked when the woman got back.

'They're leaving now. It was rather fun actually. Very amusing anyway.'

She'd had a guitar when she came in - where was it? Yes (getting up on her elbow to take the offered glass), there against the wall.

'Here, just a moment.' The woman seated herself on the edge of the bed, reached out and wiped at her face with a small clean handkerchief. 'You have been a mucky pup.' And looked carefully into her eyes a moment before getting up again. 'Drink that and you'll feel much better.'

'Thank you.' She swallowed the bitter, gritty grains, handed the glass back. There was a little silence and again she was embarrassed, didn't know what to say. As a rule, she wasn't easily embarrassed. But something this time. And then the woman turned away, put the glass down on the chest.

'Tell me,' she said with her back still turned, 'why were you drunk last night?'

In the wardrobe mirror, she caught sight of herself sitting here on the bed. Her thin arms, bony shoulders, drawn-up knees, and her hair all over the place. She'd an idea she gave the impression she was fragile, which she wasn't. Not over-fragile. Except that it was a dreadful wear and tear, her life now. And yet Frankie had said once she changed all the time, gave first one impression then another. Fragile one minute, awkwardly strong the next. That was what he'd said: Withdrawn. abandoned. Happy: sad. Introvert: extrovert. Female: male. All contrasts, he'd said. She wasn't sure how true it was or how it applied just now. Only felt that the impression she made was somehow to her advantage.

'I don't think for any particular reason,' she said at last. (But hell, it was an effort to talk at all, let alone work out answers.) 'Why?' she asked as an afterthought. And she'd touched on something tender because now it was the woman who was guarded. But only for a split second, and she disguised it easily.

'I wondered. You were in rather a bad way when I rescued you.'

'You didn't ought to have bothered, but thank you

anyway.' Suddenly anxious, she put her hair back from her face. 'I'm not a drunk or anything like that: it just happens now and then. To start with, I'd this reception affair before I came on here. You know how it is: someone offers you a drink and you can't refuse, and then someone else. A bad habit I guess, like cigarette smoking.'

'Oh, I see.' (But cynical.) 'Well, I must find my husband and think about getting along.'

Somehow or other she'd said the wrong thing, overstepped her mark. She wanted to apologise but wasn't sure for what, or even if an apology was necessary, and so said nothing. And the door closed quietly, and she was gone. And then she began to have this uncomfortable feeling, like she hadn't told the truth. She hadn't lied exactly, but maybe she hadn't told the truth either. So hell. Who wanted the truth anyway?

Carefully, she put her legs over the edge of the bed. Her clothes were crumpled, and she'd no shoes. She couldn't think what she'd done with her shoes. She hunted about a bit, looking here and there, but then remembered she'd left them in the car. They'd begun to hurt her, and she preferred to drive barefoot anyway.

She pulled the curtains, put the light off. And stood a moment, not sure what she had to do next. She saw the white grits clinging to the cloudy sides of the aspirin glass, went to the chest. It was a pretty looking-glass he had. Who did that disc jockey guy say he was? Oh yeah. An art gallery, somewhere in the West End. (She liked that: said it over again to herself. West End.) Yeah, Graffman. She remembered now. He'd all her records, loved her voice. That was all she knew. Which was more than she knew about the disc jockey. Him: she didn't even know his name. Didn't want to either. Those people, they made her sick. And the Gould guy too, the one who brought her here. (They'd left the other place without telling Cassidi or anyone.) There was this about Englishmen: they never grew up. Just like kids.

She gave the glass a little push and her reflection jumped up at her. Her face was dirty and there was a white, scar like seam along her jaw where the saliva had taken the dirt with it. Her hair was tangled, and all runched up at the back, and there was a livid indentation in her bare arm where her bracelet had cut in while she slept. She had a blocked look still: her eyes only half open, like she'd been smoking pot. It scared her a bit, the way she looked. Five years ago, when she first went on the folksong kick, she was seventeen. Now, this minute, in the glass, she looked twice that. But it would wear off shortly, it always did. An hour or two, and she'd be all right.

Yeah, next she had to go outside. And then she had to get away from here, had to get back to her hotel. Cassidi had said to be ready at ten. But, about to leave the room, she saw the handbag. There, on the chair. She went back, set the guitar down again. Then, too interested to let a twinge of conscience bother her, she quickly opened the bag and checked the contents. Nothing much. A lipstick, paper hankies, a key, a comb, a small mirror and a pair of black gloves. Oh and a card: Anthony Stankovich, in small black letters, and the address and phone number. Hampstead? Where was that? She looked again at the card. N.W.11.

'North West Eleven,' she said aloud in a doubtful, negative sort of way. Then shut the bag, left it where she'd found it. (But she wished she hadn't said to the woman about people offering you a drink and not being able to refuse and about it being a bad habit. It was a lie, or at best a half truth, and misrepresentative. It made it seem like she was some kind of boastful kid or something - she hated to think about it.)

There was nobody about, not a sound. The place was dead quiet. (God knows what happened to Gould: he must have gone.) She went into the lavatory first, then slowly downstairs and out into the early morning light. In the square, the birds were singing. She could smell the moist, warm smell of the ground there, let the air blow on her face before stowing the guitar in the luggage space. Someone had scrawled all over the windscreen in lipstick. We love Sarah: Susan, Jenny, and Stasia. (They'd been at the party she supposed, whoever they were.) And three lipstick kisses. She tried to get it off with a Kleenex tissue, but it messed it all up. She left it, slipped into the driving seat and banged the door. The car was a loan: friends she'd made last visit. Friend rather. A specially well off young man - his daddy had thousands stashed away in the bank - called Stephen. He dabbled in pop and politics, depending on what mood he was in. And queer as a coot, but a nice guy. For the whole of her stay, the car was hers. He'd garaged it at the hotel for her soon as he knew she was due to arrive. If he needed it, he'd come and get it. No, not at all: not to mention it. The pleasure was his. (All in that crazy English way of talking.) She sat in the car a minute, then drank from a flask she kept in her handbag. Had to get hold of it with both hands, and shaking a little, but was better after. Then glanced quickly through the rear window, took the long low bonnet round in a tight turn and trod on the accelerator.

SARAH

She left the car in the square and, a bit guilty because she'd stolen the time, given Cassidi the slip again, investigated her way into the side streets. The sun shone bright and hot: all these people were busy doing something. She didn't, in any case, really think she'd get recognised. That was one of the good things about being famous: people didn't recognise you. Not unless you tried for it. (And there were too many copies. People couldn't be sure. At a party once someone had gone up to a girl standing right next to her, and looking as much like her as was possible, and said was she Sarah Kumar?) One had to go certain places if one wanted to be recognised. And especially in London. She felt safer in London than anywhere else in the world. People weren't so curious. Or, if they were, didn't want to seem curious. And she'd got these shades on in any case. She felt a bit of a phoney, going about in shades, but they made it that bit more difficult if somebody did get curious.

There were barrows and barber shops and theatrical agencies and wine shops and shops where they sold a hundred varieties of sausage or cheese. There were so many people she didn't feel the least bit conspicuous: her shadow fell flat and dark before her just like anybody else's. The sun was almost directly overhead, burned her bare shoulders, glanced back off the pavement, and dithered over the coloured awnings of the barrows. Now, in spite of the glasses, she was dazzled, now the dark angle of a building at the street corner cut across her vision. First she had to screw her eyes against the light, then she was plunged in darkness and felt the cool of the shadow and couldn't see a thing. And she hadn't thought it could be so hot in England. Leastways, not this time of year. Last visit, it had rained all the time.

Here she crossed the street, and into the shadow again. She looked at the fruit on a barrow slung up at the edge of the pavement: bananas, pears and apples in neat rows, and peaches. Imported, she guessed. The peaches were firm and large and such a warm, sunny colour. (They grew in her garden back home.) So she put it to the test, her anonymity, bought three. Nothing happened of course. The skinny-necked little man who wore no collar hardly looked at her. But she was left with the peaches, and nowhere to put them. Only inside. She could have eaten the lot she was so hungry now. (Only a cup of tea at the studio.) But difficult in a street full of people, and everybody so good at pushing. (She didn't really mind this: it made a change from being on her own anyway.)

She turned the corner. The sun hit at her again. Her head still thumped a bit after last night, and all those hot lights at the studio hadn't helped much. Someone had trod on a tomato there in the gutter and it seemed to her suddenly her head must look something like that inside and the thought drove her into the espresso bar just here on her left. She'd get herself a coffee. No, not a coffee. She didn't like it anyway. A pineapple juice or something. Yes. Cool and sharp. She got a shock all the same when she went in and heard the folk-rock ballad she'd cut to coincide with this visit. (There was a transistor radio among the fruit juices and things on the shelf.) Her company here had released it specially, but they'd aired it to death already on the pirate stations. But the same shock she always got when she heard herself, or saw a pic of herself, unexpected. Like a bogy had jumped out at her. She felt suddenly exposed, betrayed, naked of everything. And would have gone out again, only the white-jacketed Italian at the bar asked did the signorina want coffee?

She shook her head, but was too distracted to smile.

'No, pineapple juice. Could you put two in the glass?'

She hadn't got used to the change yet: it seemed to have gone all dark after the sunlight outside. All she could see momentarily was the Italian's white jacket and the shiny chrome of the coffee machine. And a distorted picture of herself in the machine, like a peep into another world. Attenuated brown arms and silver bangles on her wrist, her hair longer than long, and the dark glasses excruciatingly large. She thought to take them off, but then didn't want to risk it. Nobody knew she was here: she'd crept in, unheralded, hoping to get some shopping done. Still.

The place was small and crowded but there was one seat vacant over the other side. She didn't want to stand at the bar, so she took it. There was a narrow formica ledge crowded with used cups, and there was a small bowl of brown sugar. And on the wall was a long glass which she avoided looking into because it seemed like, if she did, she would give herself away somehow, like Jesus kissed by Judas, and everyone would recognise her at once. And shrank, too, from the amplified sound of her own voice. (Like they knew it was her, had turned the damned thing up specially.) She hadn't been too happy with that disc anyway, it was so commercial. And her real fans, the ones who were going to stay with her later, didn't want that sort of thing. And these high stools were horrible because her dress kept leaving her knees bare and awkward, and the feeling of having her knees bare in public was worse than anything she could think of. It made her feel cheap, the way men made her feel cheap.

At her elbow was an open page with its small signs and symbols all neatly set out. And then some sudden instinct made her look in the glass to see who was reading. And it was her, Mrs Stankovitch. But all wrong here: who'd have thought to find her here? The last place in the world. She was surprised but not surprised. Not surprised because she'd never felt London as a big place, not after flying in from half across the world. Surprised because, somehow, she just didn't fit. (How was she to explain that?) And that was all. And maybe was embarrassed momentarily, because the first thing she wanted to do was get up and leave. But then thought she ought to say something, but said nothing. Only looked at her. Yeah, different. She was so different. And maybe knew she was different, the way she had her nose buried in the book but didn't seem to be reading at all. And oddly unlike the person she'd seen last night: the same but not the same. Maybe because she hadn't looked at her properly before: maybe because she didn't have all that make-up on. But still she had this something beautiful going for her. She looked, right now, a bit like an old photo she'd seen once of an actress called Mrs Patrick Campbell. (Would she know of Mrs Patrick Campbell?) But fair. And didn't have that sweet, sentimental, buttoned-up little mouth fashionable then. But reading what? She couldn't quite see. But then, sensing her interest maybe, she looked up suddenly. Like she'd reached out and touched her.

'Oh, hello,' she said. But like she wasn't a bit surprised,

expected her even. But cool. Not specially pleased to see her. And, soon as the words were spoken, it was like some kind of mist or vapour stole over the whole of her, and cold, and everything was terrible. Everything that just a minute ago had been so friendly: the yellow juice in her glass, the soft mound of dark sugar, the hissing, whining coffee machine, the bright rectangle of the open door and all the people passing in the street. And that thing on the radio just jangled stupidly on. She'd have stopped it if she could, it embarrassed her so.

'You left your handbag,' she said. And equally cool in spite of it all hurting inside. 'Did you get it?'

'Yes.' And paused. 'John rang me this morning.' And then, with a kind of humour: 'Is this you?' Meaning the radio.

She was angry, yes, angry. And couldn't hide this something or other that was growing all over her like a skin. A sort of hostility, though she didn't want to be that way.

'No. This is me: here.'

'Of course. But what are you doing here?' - showing some surprise at last, and apparently prepared to ignore her rudeness.

'I only just got away from the studio,' she said, looking into her glass. 'Right now I'm supposed to be lunching with someone - we've yet to fix up what songs I'll sing this time - but I wanted to be on my own a while. I wanted to see Soho. I didn't see it properly last time.'

'Oh.'

'I'm surprised I saw you here.'

'Yes.' Slowly. 'I'm waiting for my husband actually. I'm meeting him for lunch.'

'I guess that explains it then.' Wasn't he a painter or something? She remembered someone telling her about him. 'What does he do?'

'He's a sculptor. In between teaching at art school.'

'Oh.' She twiddled her glass: it had misted up, the juice was so cold.

'How do you feel now?'

'Better, thank you.'

'And the television show - how did it go?'

'Pretty well considering. Considering you can spend hours hanging about waiting for this and that - there was always a technical fault last show I did here. But today was all right: we did a run-through, and then went right ahead and recorded it. It was just a ten-minute spot: not like doing a whole show.' She frowned a little. 'But how did you know? Who said I'd be at the television studios?'

'John, I think. Yes, John. You must have said something to him.'

Mrs Stankovich stirred her coffee. She looked at the coffee, and then at Mrs Stankovich. Carefully, because she didn't want her to know she was looking at her. She wore a silk head-scarf and a sheepskin coat. The coat was open. She thought she sensed a certain reserve, a certain caution. She wished she hadn't been so defensive, so off-hand, knew she owed her an apology but hadn't the least idea how she could manage it without loss of pride. Anyone else, she wouldn't have bothered. But she'd been so kind, had maybe spared her a lot of embarrassment last night. 'I'm sorry if it seemed I was rude just now. I hope you'll excuse me.'

'Oh, nonsense.' She meant it too, was ready to forgive. 'I'd forgotten all about it.'

And now everything shifted back into perspective. Nothing was terrible any more. Everything fitted again, like in a jigsaw puzzle accidentally wrecked. But she was careful, like she was with almost everybody, couldn't be completely sure. What to say? What not to say?

'It's difficult,' she said suddenly, not certain why she said it or what she meant by it.

'Difficult?'

'Yeah, everything. Nothing is easy: I guess that was what I meant.'

Mrs Stankovich was silent a moment, seemed to think it over.

'I'd imagine it depends on the problem,' she said at last. 'Have you a problem?'

It struck her as somehow quaint, the way she said that. Like in the ladies magazines: have you a problem? - so write to me.

'Not a particular problem. Just problems. Like most people I guess.' She'd been on the verge, she realised, of saying a whole lot of things one couldn't possibly say in a coffee bar. Things she'd not have said to anyone else, anywhere. But then she changed her mind. 'It gets kind of lonely,' she explained, thinking this might do instead. (But it was so terribly corny, all that lonely bit. Not at all what she wanted to say, but better than nothing, and one got so used in any case to talking like this - she'd not realised till just this minute how she'd got into the way of talking the corny kind of crap one talked in show business.) 'At the hotel I mean. It can be pretty boring. Usually, when I'm at a hotel, I stay in bed all day. If I don't have anything lined up, that is. I'm never warm enough, and nothing to do. I read comic papers, and keep my socks on. England

22

is so cold - I mean, most of the time. And since you can't go out you might as well stay in bed. I've a suite looks out on the river. You can see the boats and things, and it's very pretty at night. But lonely all the same.'

'Yes, I can imagine. When do you arrive officially? - John said something about your not having arrived yet according to the books.'

'Officially I arrive on Tuesday.'

But it was strong, the need to tell this particular person everything that had ever happened to her. Never, not once in her life, had anyone given her this feeling before. It was like this person was a cool, clear stream of water and she could jump in and wash herself clean of everything. She was looking for a religion maybe: and here it was. As simple as that. You had to have faith in something, or there was nothing. Everybody she'd met till now - though she'd not seen it this way before, she liked most people - they were so unreal. Cardboard people with backs and fronts but nothing inside.

'I wonder could I be rude again and ask myself over sometime? This evening maybe? I've so little time here, know so few English people - you are English, aren't you? I mean, Stankovich –?'

'Oh yes. Originally my husband's people came from Russia, but years and years ago.'

'Sounds weird I know, but most of the people I've met here aren't English at all. Or only half. I like English people but I don't know any. Or am I rude, asking like that? Most English people, I know, think Americans are terribly rude.'

'Are you American? Well, obviously you are. What I mean is you don't look like an American.'

'Yeah, well I'm not. I was born in India. I left when I was about two. My mother is Indian and my father part Indian, part British. I don't seem to have any real nationality, any positive identity - do you know what I mean? I've been all over the place but don't feel I belong anywhere.'

'Perhaps that's the reason?'

'Maybe. But I don't like nationality anyway. I don't want to be American any more than I want to be Indian or British or anything else. But you have to be something, so I guess I'm an Indian. Or maybe not because my parents are naturalised Americans now. But that depends too.'

'Depends on what?'

'On who we're talking to. Back home, most people seem to think we're the wrong colour for Americans. You only have to be the least bit brown, and we're more than that. America likes her Americans Omo white - don't you have a wash powder called that?'

'Yes. Yes, we have.'

Mrs Stankovich wouldn't comment further. She was sceptical maybe? Or simply embarrassed? She couldn't, in any case, let her get away with it.

'Blanco, you know? It's sad though, the way things are back home. It's a wrong approach - there didn't ought to have to be an approach anyway. It makes for a false awareness in the minds of peoples who'd never have seen it as a problem otherwise.'

'That's true of course,' Mrs Stankovich agreed. (But was careful of this kind of talk. Maybe she thought she talked like a book, put it too consciously - maybe she did, she'd said the same thing so many times, had got so used to shouting in deaf ears.) 'Anyway,' smiling suddenly, 'it doesn't worry me in the least what colour people are so perhaps you'd like to come this evening? I'm sure my husband would be most interested to meet you. I'm having a few people to dinner though - would you mind? John, for one. He's fetching me my handbag back.'

'Oh no. That's all right. Where do I go?'

'Here, take my card. Anthony's rather. But the address is there. Will you find it all right?'

She felt a bit guilty, seeing the card. She read the address through twice, aloud the second time, then nodded.

'Yes, I think so. So all I have to do tonight is get away on my own. Not always easy: I have my personal manager with me, Harry Cassidi. He's okay, but terribly scared for me. Doesn't like me to go about on my own. He's afraid after tomorrow they'll have me deported or something.'

'Good heavens, I hope not. What are you getting up to tomorrow?'

'Oh it doesn't matter.'

'No, I'd like to hear about it.'

'Only that your CND asked me last time I was over would I march with them? I wasn't able then, but I promised I'd do something next time. Harry says I didn't ought to, but it's one promise I'm keeping.'

'But you say officially you've not arrived yet?'

'That's right.'

'Then you can't be in two places at once?'

'I don't aim to be.'

'Perhaps, though, your Mr Cassidi has a point. Those meetings are pretty rowdy affairs, and the Press will know you when they see you if no one else does.'

'Too bad. I'm not bothered.'

'Isn't it a little early though? I thought these things took place during the holiday?'

'Well yes. But since I couldn't be here then we had to arrange it like this. This doesn't have anything to do with the Easter march though: they'll have that anyway I guess. This is a protest against American policy in Vietnam, you know?'

Mrs Stankovich smiled a little, shrugged her shoulders. 'So long as you're happy about it. Why don't you take those glasses off?'

'Why?'

'So that I can see you better, that's all. I'm not sure what sort of person you are behind them.'

'No, I can't.'

'Will you wear them on the march too?'

'You're laughing at me.'

'No.'

'I shan't be alone on the march. There's safety in numbers. Anyhow, what time can I come tonight?'

'Seven?'

'Yeah, fine.' (But she had to get rid of this feeling, this fence she'd put up when she asked why didn't she take the shades off.) 'Will you excuse me now, only I have this lunch date. Cassidi's going to be mad when he sees me: he already blasted me once today. And this afternoon I have to do some shopping. I want to get some clothes: you've some cool things in the shops here.'

'Yes, certainly.'

'I'm late already, but I have the car - my meter will have run out too I guess. The only English person I know really well loaned me this car while I'm here. It's no fun driving in London though: I haven't opened the throttle once.'

'Oh London is useless, I agree. One might as well ride a bicycle.'

'Yeah, I hadn't thought of that. Good-bye then.'

'Good-bye.'

JANE

She was left with a sense of disruption, of severance. The girl had gone, but something of her remained. Someone else had taken her seat: and it was almost a shock, the dissimilarity. This whatever it was she had: quite indefinable.

Oh, she'd left something. A brown paper bag. She appropriated it quickly, afraid someone else would take it, glanced inside. Peaches, of all things. What on earth was she doing buying peaches? And, seeing them, she saw again those bare arms and legs. On one arm she wore a silver bangle: she could still see how it had looked against the colour of her skin. And a ring on her right hand. Quite plain: a gold signet ring. Slim, strong wrists - that was what she'd seen first, suddenly aware someone was watching her. And that incipient hair on the forearms usual in dark women. The glasses had confused her momentarily, but the mouth was unmistakable. Like some sort of thin-skinned fruit, a little crumpled, and broken, but resilient too, firm. Yes: rather like a too ripe tomato, but that wasn't putting it at all well. And that lift, that sudden flare of the upper lip. And the hair. Her hair was a rather beautiful brown colour, verging on red, and dark. The terracotta tints merged somehow with her complexion, accentuating the tobacco tones. But extremely reserved in her manner, though she'd got her to speak a little about herself. Not unusual she supposed: young women were always so secretive. But something more. A certain unwillingness, almost a determination to let no one in. She'd all the painful dignity of a young woman. And, in spite of her femininity, that bisexual quality most young women had. But something: something wrong somewhere. A man? Possibly. She was far too attractive to have escaped admiration. That smile, and a certain gentility. There were two kinds of smile actually. (She quite delighted to remember these things.) That slight, mysterious upward turn of the lips, and then that open, very frank and rather large smile. Like a street boy - those she'd seen in Spain. She'd a certain innocence too - a certain gladness, that was it. And all mixed with a sort of instinctive wisdom. And that impression of sharing a secret with herself so typical of young women. All those peculiar qualities older women envied, regretted. And yet she didn't envy her, felt none of that aggressive rivalry one sometimes felt with a younger woman. She was content to admire. Felt, rather, desperately sorry for her.

'Darling?'

She turned quickly.

'Oh yes. Shall we go?'

'What the devil are those?'

'Peaches.'

'Peaches?'

'Yes.' She'd been going to say she'd bought them - why, she couldn't think. 'Someone left them. Finders, keepers.'

JANE

She took off one of her earrings, held it a moment in the palm of her hand.

'What did you think of her?'

In the glass, she saw the yellow arc thrown by the bedside lamp and her husband about to step into his pyjamas. That nakedness she'd always so admired - but what did she love in him? Did she love him at all? Yes, naturally. But passion? No, not now. All that was finished. But the same tastes, the same understanding.

'I don't know. A bit enigmatic.'

'Enigmatic?' She thought a moment. 'Yes, I know what you mean. But not completely. That is, not deliberately. She's so terribly honest - didn't you feel that?'

'Her politics didn't quite make sense. All cockeyed.'

'I wasn't actually thinking of that, but I don't entirely agree with you anyway. A bit misguided perhaps, but absolutely sincere. She absolutely believed everything she said.'

'Rather beautiful anyway, in a sort of way. A very interesting looking woman' - drawing tight the string of his pyjamas, feeling carefully for the comfort of his genitals. 'I shan't put the jacket on, it's too warm.'

'Hardly a woman, darling.' But no jealousy, not a twinge. A curiosity, rather, with regard to what he thought. Not the opinion of her husband at all, but that of a close friend - that was how she saw it.

'Then what? Well into her twenties I'd have thought.'

'Twenty-two.' Carefully. And putting aside the earring now, placing it exactly - so. Afraid he might wonder at her interest, that she'd bothered to discover her age. (Oh but it was ridiculous, the way one hummed and hahed over these things. Why on earth should she be ashamed of her interest in a member of her own sex?) No, no reaction at all. (Men, in any case, were so unperceptive, so unsubtle.) He sat down on the bed, rubbed hard at his feet, each foot alternately. But this, she thought suddenly, was what she hated about marriage. A man's cold feet, the way he gradually dropped all reservations, the way he quickly got so used to one it didn't matter anymore. Nothing. Socks, underwear, all the rest.

'Girl, then.' He turned his head suddenly. She felt caught out, looked away. 'What did you say she was, American?'

'Partly. But she was born in India.'

'She's very sculptural. I said she should model. She promised she'd come and see the art school sometime, was very interested. I was telling her about the students' exhibition and so on.'

'Did she like your work - did you show her anything?'

'Yes. I don't know. Her way of smiling I think, and not saying much. She passed her hand over one or two pieces and smiled, but I wasn't sure what she meant by it. She seemed to be thinking of something else.'

She, too, smiled. Yes, she caught herself at it: there in the glass. As though enjoying some private joke.

'You gave her a cigar - not good for her voice I'd have thought?'

'She smoked one anyway.'

It had surprised her a little, delighted her too. There was something now about cigar smoke: she'd never smell it again without remembering her surprise. And the flare of the match in the girl's face. It was the face, she'd thought, of an opium dreamer - veiled, as it temporarily was, in bluish smoke. The eyelids. And the painful, lambent candour of her look. She'd this way of looking at one suddenly: wide eyed, as though into a strong light. And an urgency, a kind of desperation in the look that said help me, get me out of this dream. Or so it had seemed to her tonight. She painted her eyes perhaps? She wasn't sure. Only that sometimes they seemed large, other times not so large.

There was a short silence while she removed the other earring and then got up and came across to the bed.

'I think John was rather surprised to find her here. Did you see the way he looked momentarily? As though he couldn't believe his eyes. Rather amusing I thought. He likes her very much.'

'Frankly, I didn't know what to expect. What does one expect of a pop singer?' He swung his legs up and drew the clothes over him. 'I noticed she drinks a bit.'

She wanted very much to put up a defence for her, but it was true. One couldn't help noticing. Why though? Any of a thousand reasons she supposed.

'You know what it is with those people: I expect one gets into the habit. But I keep telling you, darling, she's not a pop singer. Not at all the same thing. Did you also notice she has yellow eyes? Well, not yellow. But honey coloured, something like that.'

'No.'

But had he? She suspected him suddenly, thought perhaps he'd rather keep it to himself. (But, God knows, she was used enough to his infidelities.) She slipped off her clothes, got into bed. He reached out his hand and switched off the light. They both of them lay quite still, and he rambled on a while about the evening in general. And then said good night, turned over. No embrace. They seldom embraced now. Her fault, she knew. But she couldn't be what she wasn't. Years ago, at the beginning, she'd wanted children. But what with one thing and another: Anthony's work, her own social interests. And she'd drawn him rather into her world. He enjoyed her connections, the continuous invitations to this, that and the other. It had helped him a lot too. And somehow the time had just slipped away, and now they were both a lot older, and had got into a way of behaving almost without noticing it. She would think suddenly: good heavens, I could have had a grown-up daughter or son now. And regretted it. But then there was this to do and that to do, so much to think of all the time. And again she forgot. And so it went on.

'I went to convent school. Theoretically there was no segregation - it's not Christian, is it? But among the kids. You know what kids are like.'

This much she'd got out of her: a brief history of her background. That she'd gone to convent school, that she'd gone on to college, that she'd left because she just wasn't that kind of person. She wasn't an intellectual, and that was that. Her parents had been disappointed, yes, but hadn't tried to influence her in any way. She'd wanted to sing, had taught herself to play the guitar, and then it happened. Yes, she liked singing folksongs but the 'boom' didn't interest her. Financially it was good for her but the charts and that - she wasn't bothered. She didn't exactly dislike the ballyhoo, but it was stupid, 'Best I like your traditional songs, but they don't want me to do that type of song now. My manager I mean. Because of the boom.

I enjoy doing folk-rock numbers: I don't have any musical prejudices. But I love traditional songs, and I'd like to play serious music too. Experiment a little. My brother is very interested in music, plays around with all sorts of instruments.'

She'd a brother who'd married a black girl and gone to live in Paris. Things were too difficult at home. Her parents hadn't minded in the least, but other people turned funny.

She was in London only till Wednesday - well, Thursday morning. In between she had that television show, the one she'd recorded this morning, a recording session, and Wednesday she was playing a concert at the Royal Festival Hall. The only one she was doing this time. He'd wanted another tour, Cassidi, but she'd refused. She then flew to Paris, where she was playing the Paris Olympia. They were buying her records fast in France, were wild about her, and she hadn't been there yet. After Paris she was doing gigs all over the country, then Paris again, then straight back home. Oh, and the march, of course, tomorrow. Though, like she said, they were all against it. Cassidi particularly. He thought it was bad publicity. (Yeah, he got so worried about her last visit he put a tail on her: it had nearly been the end of their beautiful friendship.) He didn't in any case see the point, if it was publicity she wanted, for doing it before her official arrival date. She'd tried to make them see, Cassidi, all of them, she wasn't just loaning them her name. She didn't care if nobody knew who she was. She was marching with them, not for them. Oh and play, play, play. All the time. If she wasn't sleeping, or eating, or anything else, she was playing. There wouldn't be any new numbers though, not this time. They'd decided this morning to stick to the old ones on account of her only just having caught on here, and people expecting to hear the ones they knew. So it wasn't like she had to learn any new numbers. Meantime, she cracked her knuckles to keep her fingers supple. She'd had trouble with her fingers since the beginning: they were nice and long but stiff at the knuckles. She was always cracking them to keep them supple. When she'd learned the piano at school they'd said her wrists were good, nice and easy, but her fingers were no good at all.

'I hope the weather keeps for you tomorrow,' she'd said, seeing her out. Hadn't been able to think of anything more intelligent: politics bored her anyway. But then Anthony, cynical as always, had wanted to know wasn't she afraid it'd be a bit rowdy?

Yes she'd heard they were often rowdy, and it upset her when she heard bad reports. But wasn't it true that those sort of people were attracted to every kind of public meeting, that they came only to make trouble?

This was exactly what he'd had in mind, Anthony said.

It was a pity, she'd agreed. It was bad publicity for them too, the CND kids. Nobody was going to take them seriously if they behaved badly. But, smiling suddenly, she wasn't at all afraid. And maybe this time it'd be different.

But they were a dying organization, the CND, didn't she know? They'd little or no influence. He doubted they knew what pacifism was, they behaved so irresponsibly.

She thought a moment then said she simply didn't believe this was true. And, hardening a little, nothing was going to stop her tomorrow anyway.

A wonderful accident, she'd explained to John just

after. I was waiting for Anthony: we were going to have lunch. And in she came.

SARAH

Time they got to the Square, a lot of people of all kinds had joined the procession. All sorts of weird sorts of people. Either out of real curiosity or to laugh at them. It poured with rain. It had poured all morning. She was drenched. The Square was packed and all around the Square, on the steps of Saint Martin's Church and the National Gallery, a lot more people stopped to look. The monument was all draped with huge, sodden black banners bearing CND slogans and symbols. To end the war in Vietnam: sing for peace in Vietnam. And a couple of kids up on the steps organising the mikes and that. The sky, all changing greys, looked like only the column kept it up: a black, Herculean arm.

A little yellow helicopter airplane flew chutter chutter round the column a few times, the sound of its engine coming and going on the wind. She didn't know why it was there: it didn't make sense. Nothing made sense today. And the rain kept on coming.

When the procession appeared, walking east from the Marble Arch, she was recognised at once. (She'd a feeling someone must have spread it around already.) The kids all shouted for her, and waved like mad, and then a whole crowd began chanting her name over and over. She didn't think she'd get through, had lost sight of the ardent spectacled guy who carried her guitar. A raw wind blew right across the Square, rushed in her face then whipped around and bore against her back. The rain, all angry and sharp like needles, stung her bare face and hands. She saw the yellow-white of her knuckles like they didn't belong to her, her hands were so cold. Her hair, blown about and wet, pasted itself across her face so she couldn't see a thing or went anywhere else the wind took it with a furious abandon.

A lot of policemen running clip clop, clip clop. She couldn't hear the clip clop, but it looked like that. One had caught hold of her arm and was forcing a way for her through the crowd. Hands shot out on all sides, caught at her clothes and hair. Touching her like for a benediction, like she was some kind of holy person.

'There's a guy somewhere back there with my instrument,' she said to the policeman. 'I don't know where he's got to.'

'It's all right, Miss. He's coming behind.'

She thought just then the policeman was the nicest person she'd met today: she'd have liked to jump right inside his tunic and be buttoned in safe and secure. But here were the lions, and some kids scrambling all over them, and policemen dragging them down as fast as they got up. Up down, up down, kicking and shouting. Woops, that one just lost his trousers. They'd tried to put up a slogan of their own, but that was pulled down too. But all she was thinking was she hoped to God her instrument would be all right. She wished she'd brought the other, the newer one.

She reached the safety of the platform, along with the organisers, feeling a bit pulled about - her arm ached like anything. All around, the Square rocked with people. It rocked and swelled and the rain, coming down straight now, seemed to weld them all into a black mass. They didn't care about the rain: neither did she. But, all in a lump like this, they worried her a little. It was a lot more frightening than being up on a stage, and there were some who hadn't come to hear anyone sing let alone Sarah bloody Kumar. She saw a placard or two: something about keeping Britain white. (One of the boys who'd helped to organise the march was a West Indian.) A whole gang of them, down there on the right. The ones who'd kept being dragged down off the lion. She didn't know if they'd got wind of her attendance previously, or what. But they knew who she was because of her name being shouted out and that, and called out she was just another bloody nigger. What was so stupid was it hadn't got anything to do with the meeting: they were just looking for trouble. But she slipped the strap over her head and the spectacled boy adjusted the mike for her. They'd stopped chanting and were clapping and cheering, and some booing there on the right. (There'd been a time when she'd had a thing about the law: she was glad of it right now.) One of them called out to her to shut up and go back home. But drowned in a new burst of cheering as she picked out some preliminary chord shapes. She didn't know how good the equipment was, if she'd make herself heard or not. When the cheering stopped even, because the wind snatched the sound away soon as it came. (The whirlybird had gone though, chuttered away in the direction of the river.) The sky was changing all the time: now light, now dark, and both together. But everything else mostly black. And twenty thousand faces all turned in her direction. Soon as she began to sing though, the atmosphere was great. They loved her. Yeah this is great, she kept telling herself. (So wasn't it?) A song made popular by giants like Pete Seeger and Joan Baez. (She'd been going to say something about that but changed her mind. She wondered anyway if she hadn't taken on too much with this song.) A Hard Rain's a Gonna Fall.

And when she came to the bit where it said about the rain falling, that it would fall hard, she looked up at the sky suddenly and they all laughed out loud. (It was calculated maybe, but nobody seemed to mind about that.) Till, signing she couldn't go on, they were quiet again.

And through with it. And then, when she'd finished, she thought she ought to say something.

'I don't know if you've noticed, but most folksongs have a message of some kind.' She smiled suddenly, drew the plectrum gently across the strings. 'Messages of all kinds.' A gust of laughter, dragged away on the wind. 'I'm going to sing you a Malvina Reynolds song. It doesn't say about Vietnam maybe, but the feeling is there. It's a song I value specially because it says about freedom. Before I begin though, I'd like to say this about peace: peace is loving one another, and it's up to each of us to keep this in mind.' She paused, then added as an afterthought: 'That man Jesus knew what he was talking about.'

'Ah shut up.'

She waited till it was quiet, not looking at anyone in particular, her head bent. Then began again. And a good beaty accompaniment.

There was some disturbance while she went through with it: catcalls and indecencies. Someone down there had blown up a big pink balloon that had MAYBE daubed on it in black paint, and when she started on the third verse they let the air slowly and loudly out the balloon and this sparked off a sudden eruption, an exchange of blows. A boy was taken away, and then more kicks and punches. Others craned their necks in the direction of the scuffle, shouted for silence. The whole close-packed mass wobbled, pressed forward, and the scuffle spread, ran out like ripples on a pond. She was fighting a losing battle trying to make herself heard. Exasperated, unsure, she stopped.

'What goes on?'

'I think perhaps they don't like us,' the West Indian boy explained.

'You can say that again.'

'It'll be all right in a minute,' the boy with the glasses apologised.

'I'm thinking different.'

And the words were only just out of her mouth when suddenly the mob broke loose. Some had managed to get up on to the platform. Her first thought was to get out fast, but then she remembered she wasn't here for that. And in any case, turning to go she nearly knocked herself out against the West Indian boy who looked like he wondered what hit him.

'Don't hit anybody, don't make a fight,' she said to the boy with glasses, but he'd already struck out. He missed. So then this other guy got hold of him like he was nothing and smashed his glasses into his face. She saw the blood begin to come. He stood a moment, then his eyes went into the middle and he fell like a log. She was going to help him if she could but then someone shouted out to get the niggers and one of them got the West Indian boy and the other got her. The guitar was snatched from her

39

and thrown down the steps bong bong and whoever it was had hold of her pulled her round suddenly and thrust her face into the wall of the pediment. Pain somewhere. Her nose? Her mouth? And for a minute it was like the wall was rushing away from her, the whole thing crashing, and she didn't know if she was happy or sad. Angrily, passionately happy she thought - or maybe she was kidding herself? But then a couple of policemen had hold of her again, were rushing her off somewhere. All she seemed to do today was be rushed backwards and forwards acoss the Square with her feet clawing for something to tread on, her eyes wild and staring and her breath coming and going in gasps like an early movie heroine. A camera bulb flared in her face. Everything was white, then violet, then black again. The Square seethed with riot: she was crushed, battered, knocked about, fought over. There were pink balloons everywhere, and people jumping in and out the fountains like anything. And a pain in her face like nobody's business. She could just as easily have laughed or cried, it wouldn't have mattered which. She wasn't sure yet what she felt, except perhaps the indignity of being manhandled all the way across the Square. And next she knew she was out of the crowd, had changed hands, and was sitting in a taxi cab with Harry Cassidi. (She liked him better than the policeman even just then, but wouldn't have said so for anything.) People were milling about the cab, snatched at the door handles, but then the rain-distorted faces broke free, floated off and were left behind.

Not looking at her, he handed her his handkerchief.

'I don't know what's the matter with you. You might have been very badly hurt.'

'Yeah.'

'And now the Press. You don't want this sort of publicity.'

But smooth, his anger, soft spoken. He couldn't afford to upset her. She said nothing, drew the collar of her coat across her face. But couldn't keep her teeth from chattering, and her hand came away bloodied. And the blood all mingled with the wet of the rain, and her knuckles white. Saddened, shaken, a little embarrassed too, she huddled in the corner of the cab. She could feel the wet crawling across her scalp, and on down her neck.

'I hadn't expected it would turn out this way,' she said at last. 'I was anxious there shouldn't be any violence.'

'Lucky for you, I had. We get this sort of thing happen at home, don't we?' Not looking at her still, but out of the window.

'I guess so.' And then, getting a grip on things again: 'Where are we going anyway?'

Cassidi, sunk in his expensive overcoat, took hold of the strap as the cab went into a bend. His body swayed and swung, went with the cab like he'd never walked on two legs in all his life.

'Dear girl, to the hotel. What about your face: does it hurt much?'

SARAH

She put the phone down, went into the bathroom. (There was a phone in the bathroom too, only she hadn't gotten round to using it yet, it seemed such a funny place to have a phone. Imagine putting a call through for a ham

41

sandwich if you were sitting in the bath or shaving under your arms: she'd feel she was acting somehow indecent.) First she washed her face, then smoothed some ointment into the wound. It wasn't as bad as she'd thought. A big bruise, and the skin all broken. Peering in the glass to ascertain the effect, whether or not it'd spoil her looks for Wednesday, she tried to make sense of the affair. But it had all happened too quick: she wasn't thinking clearly yet. And anyway, like Cassidi said, she might have expected it. He'd warned her, they'd all warned her, and that was that. No good getting upset about it.

Back in the other room, she poured herself a drink. Hesitated, picked up the phone again.

'Is Mrs Stankovich there?' (Her foreign help at the other end.) 'Thanks.' (A voice somewhere, the girl's Danish accent. Calling up the stairs. And then someone coming down, and then picking up the phone.)

Yes, who was it?

'Sarah Kumar. I'm incarcerated here at the hotel. Huh? No, it was a flop. What I wanted to ask you was could you have dinner tonight? I just cancelled the other date I had a few minutes ago.'

Yes, she thought she could. (But was surprised, or seemed surprised.)

'Where?'

Well there was a place in Knightsbridge. (But not certain. Like she was doing something she shouldn't.) She'd book a table.

'What time?' She lifted the twisty cable, slipped her finger through the coil. It was all kind of cloak and dagger somehow. 'Fine. I don't suppose your husband will object?'

Good heavens no. He'd late classes tonight as it chanced. No, not a class. There were, of course, no classes today. (Laughing a little.) He was going to the school anyway. They were making up masks and things for the students' dance.

'So long then.'

But how long? Hours. That many hours too many. What an idiotic waste of time. She finished her drink, then lay down on the bed. Went into a sleep of sorts: dozing, waking, looking at the clock. The phone went once: Cassidi. Because, getting no answer, he came and knocked at her door. She made out she was asleep. (She'd been going to play some, to work out a simpler chord progression on one of the items billed for Wednesday. But hadn't the energy. Her face ached and she was tired out.) And then was woken fully by the phone going again. She got off the bed, went and picked it up.

Oh Miss Kumar? A call from Paris.

'Who?'

Mister Paul Kumar.

'Yeah, put him through.'

Sassy?

'Hi.' (And kissed over the phone like they always did.)

They weren't sure if she was in London yet. How went it?

'Fine. And you? And Stella?'

Fine. Stella wasn't there just then. She went out, but said to give her love and looking forward to seeing her. She'd be in Paris when?

'Thursday.'

Yeah. (A pause.) Guess who was in Paris? Guess who he met up with yesterday?

43

'I don't know. I can't.'

Frankie Rosengarten.

(Her heart thumped something wild. She had to take a hold on herself before she could say anything.)

'You're joking.'

No: gospel. He was there right now. Would she like to talk to him?

'Jesus, no.' (She had to keep hold of the phone with both hands she was shaking so.)

Ah not to be stupid. Come on.

'No. I don't want to.'

So what did he say to him?

(She could tell from the way he spoke he was smiling, could picture them together. They'd always been buddies. It didn't seem possible all the same, that she could have spoken to him if she'd wanted. She specially remembered walking in a field of com with him. A big, sloping field, and tall hedges all around and a path cutting through and he put his hand on her buttock as they walked. She remembered how it had felt, the feeling she'd got from that. Like his hand burned a hole in her dress. And the bond it had created between them - they'd just made up a quarrel. That peculiar man-woman bond she'd so wanted from him.)

'Say to him to bugger off or anything you like. I'm not interested.'

Never mind. (Like he was a bit embarrassed.) But she'd come and see them - him and Stella?

'Soon as I can.' (But she objected to sharing all this with Frankie Rosengarten and she couldn't be like she was before she'd known he was there.) 'How's the baby?'

Just fine. He wasn't a baby any more though. Hadn't

Stella written her? - he was walking about now. More or less. And he was this beautiful colour - like her, only more so because of Stella. (He still spoke about Stella like they'd only just got married. She felt good when she was with them, they were so happy together.)

'Kiss him right on the nose for me.'

Yeah, he'd do that.

'Maybe I'll see you Thursday. If not, Friday.'

She kissed him over the phone again, rang off. And hurt a little first, and then was angry, and then didn't give a damn. As easy as that. Just like when they were together, her and Frankie.

JANE

'Incense and candle bells, and wax polish. Every place you went you smelt wax polish. The chapel too. I specially remember the smell of the chapel. And if you put a few cents in a box you could have yourself a candle prayer. Like for your best friend if she had the measles. And the candles standing like a company of spears in the draughty flickering dark. And the negative, smiling Virgin with her outstretched hands and tears like jewels on her face. But I told you, didn't I, I went to convent school?'

'Yes.'

Subdued lights at intervals around the room, and the atmosphere rather warm. They'd a table right at the back, and just around the corner. Except for one adjoining table, they were more or less alone. Miss Kumar - but wasn't that somehow ridiculous? - Miss Kumar sat opposite, with her back to the wall. And one tall candle on the table which the waiter had lit when they sat down to their meal. And a pair of lights up there on the left: a warm, oblique glow across the wall. The candle burned between them like a pale moon, motionless. And created a kind of vacuum, a sense of everything having stopped. Time, everything. What happened outside of it was unimportant. She hardly noticed. People came and went, and that was all. Somewhere at the back of her there was a subdued murmur of conversation. Each of those persons was in more or less the same condition she supposed: each had his candle. But that was as far as it went, her interest. So that the room was hardly real, was more of a Hoffmanesque dream. These soft reds and browns and golds, and the coloured candle. A blue colour. (It was this, perhaps, reminded Miss Martinez of the Virgin?)

They'd finished their meal, sat over coffee. Coffee for her, brandy for Miss Kumar. Who was suddenly silent, poked at the candle with a matchstick and made the flame wobble. (On one side, the skin of her nose was bruised and broken. It looked rather tender.) The table was still littered with the debris of the meal. Screwed up paper napkins, fish frames - very intricate yet simple, like Chinese ivory work - a sprig of parsley, a slice of lemon, and the nearly empty carafe.

With the candlelight on her face - and, obliquely, the glow of the lights - Miss Kumar had the look of a vaguely debauched young goddess, or priestess of some sort. Those exotic bronzes and things one saw in museums. Something to do with the colour of the lights, and her being rather warm too. This oiled look her skin had: burnished, anointed. Also, her dignity. She'd this natural dignity. (Even when she remembered her vomiting into the basin at John's.) But floating somehow, disconnected. Like a lost child. (But, which made it so painful, not a child at all. A fully formed and, she would have thought, rather strong character.) And a little afraid too, though she was probably not even aware of this. Right off at a tangent, misdirected. All her goodness misdirected.

'The special tinkle of those little handbells - I still hear them sometimes, and wonder where I am. Bells of all sorts. Bells for this, bells for that.'

She watched her across the table, silent. Then said: 'What happened at the meeting this morning? I hear there was a bit of a rumpus.'

'Nothing much. A handful of stupid - you know the sort. One of them pushed my face into the wall. And my guitar: they smashed that too.' She jabbed at the wax a moment, then smiled. 'I'd a feeling I'd lost it right at the beginning. But I've another with me, so it's all right. I can't figure though how people get to hate so. I guess you have to ignore them. Wouldn't do to feel too much, there's too many of them.'

'But you do?'

'Do what?'

'You feel it.'

There was another short silence.

'You know what they called me at school?' she asked at last, as though they'd never spoken of the meeting.

'No?'

'Nigger. On account of my skin. On account of it being brown.' She shrugged. 'They don't differentiate you see: anybody brown is a nigger. It's difficult to explain the suspicion back home, and the hatred it breeds - but I told you all that already. But they gave me as bad a time as they could without it noticing too much. They stole things from me and I had to go ask for them back, and they'd say I was nuts - they hadn't anything of mine. And they'd keep this up for a while. And then one of them would say she had it so there, but I wasn't getting it back. And I used to get angry, real mad. So angry I could have killed somebody. Only I wouldn't let them know this. And they'd all look at me like they couldn't wait to see what happened next. And then one would say 'here nigger', and throw it right back at me, and they were all off as quick as they could go. Everybody can share except Sarah Kumar - you know the kind of thing. And poke me about with their elbows and then say stop pushing and then call out to teacher Sarah Kumar keeps on pushing. And I'd be made to stand up on the form for the rest of the lesson. But I never let them see how they hurt me, and I think they were all a bit puzzled and even a bit scared. You know?'

All this was spoken in an oddly negative sort of way, as though she were reading from a book. A touch of irony perhaps, but no bitterness. Not a hint of a grumble. The resignation, the passive withdrawal of the persecuted. She was glad, of course, of an audience. Was dramatic in that distant way young women were dramatic. Observed, kept track of herself - was perhaps not even conscious of doing so.

'Yes, I know.'

'I remember my first night there. I'd never been so miserable. I was about nine I think. With all my other new stuff I'd got this large tablet of scented soap. Smooth and round and green coloured. Just to smell scented soap now makes me think of cold early mornings, and cubicles and chapel and cascaras. We had those once a week: every Saturday morning. And six inches of tepid bath water before bed every night. And you had to wear something they called a bath shirt so you wouldn't see yourself naked.' She lifted a small piece of black out of the liquid wax, then said: 'First night I was there I woke up and found I'd wet the bed. I was all in a panic, didn't know what to do. But I dried it up with my Teddy bear and they never found out. Or if they did they never said. But you know, before I went to that place I was never scared of anything - not any more than other kids. Or anyone, except my parents. But I get scared sometimes now. I think I was scared at the meeting this morning. Another thing about that school: it was the first time I'd worn stockings and that and I hated it. I didn't feel old enough. I felt like they were making a woman of me before I knew what it was all about, being a woman. But you had to wear stockings, even the littlest kids, and that was that.'

'But you were happier at college? Or not?'

She sat back against the wall, took up her glass and looked into it. The long hair cast a shadow across one half of her face. She kept her eyes down, turned the glass this way and that. Musician's hands: long, interesting fingers.

'At college I did something I wish ever since I'd never done. I fell in love with one of the professors and I gave him my virginity.' She looked up suddenly. 'Same old stupid old story. But it wasn't quite my fault. He said how he loved me and how we'd be married and said there was nothing wrong about it if we were to be married. So I agreed. I wanted it anyway, I'm not saying I didn't. I loved him something awful and the best thing I could

49

think of was to sleep with him. Next day he avoided me, was cold. I couldn't make it out. So, because I was desperate, I cornered him and asked him what was the matter. I can see it now, the way he looked at me. He began to perspire: there were little beads of perspiration on his forehead and he went a funny white colour. Then he turned his back on me and said he was sorry but he couldn't marry me. His people would object, he thought, if he married me. On account of the difference, he said. What difference?, I asked. He looked at me again then, in a surprised sort of way like hadn't I ever looked in the mirror, and said good God, the difference in colour. But that I didn't mind so much. What I minded was he used this as an excuse, another way of telling me he didn't love me anyway and had never intended to marry me or anything like that, black, white or yellow.' She looked carefully at her a moment, then away again. 'I can't think of anything worse than to have given so easily what I gave. I can't ever forgive myself for having been such a fool. I know all that kind of talk is useless, but it's true. If there was something I could have, anything in the world, I'd have back what I gave to him.' She waited a while, still turning the glass. 'You didn't mind, did you, my telling you that?'

Unlike many Americans she spoke rather beautifully. Quietly. And enunciated very clearly. Only her speech was sometimes fricative, the S's particularly. Because of her teeth perhaps? It didn't matter anyway. The only doubts she had at the moment - oddly, because she'd been quite convinced of it till now - concerned the girl's sincerity. She rather felt that all this talk, this self exposure, was a bit of a confidence trick. Aimed at whipping up her sympathy. She forgave her nevertheless: young women were such actresses.

'Not at all.'

'Only you were looking at me funny: I thought maybe you were bored.'

'Nonsense.'

'But there are other things too. I've done such awful things. It's funny how, once you're in, you can't get out again. You slip once, and it's all too easy next time. When I left college and started on the folk kick I met a man called Frankie. He was a kid really, like me. A lot younger than Houston. But he was serious like Houston. He was a painter. Houston, though he treated me dirty, was a nice person. I mean he was mature, grown up. Frankie wasn't a nice person. But he was a very attractive person. He had a very pretty body, small and like a boy. If I wore high heels it made me taller than him so I never wore them. I don't like them anyway. But I remember how perfect his body was - I'd never seen such a pretty man. I lived with him three years. I worshipped him, like he was a little god or something. He looked like one anyway, when he was naked. Like an Eros.'

Miss Kumar reached for her glass, saw it was empty. And was going to sign to the waiter, but she interrupted her.

'Are you driving? Didn't you come by car?'

'Oh. Yeah.'

But as though she hadn't heard. She poked at the candle again, doubtfully, and her eyes were large in the candle light, yellow-brown. They had this wide, candid look which was oddly at variance with what she was telling about herself. But that it was true, she didn't doubt: it was all there in her face.

'He wasn't of course - a god I mean. Much less than that. He was a neurotic, and selfish and mean. If I went to him and he didn't want me he'd put up his arm and knock me the other side of the room. He'd do that all the time - make out he wanted me, and then hit me. I gave him as good though - I had to, though inside I was terrified of him. And then he'd burst into tears, and I'd sit on the floor with him and cry too. And then it was all right with him for a few days. But he had this mean temper, you know? And suddenly he'd stop speaking to me, and it'd go something like this: "All right, if you don't want to talk to me I don't want to talk to you either." And then, about half an hour later: "Frankie, don't you want to talk to me?" Once, just to see what he'd say, I told him I was pregnant. He punched me right in the mouth, it scared him so. It would have done him good to have had to face some sort of responsibility, he was such a little boy, so selfish. I think he only had me because he thought he ought to have a woman. Not because he loved me. When he had sex with me I could tell he hated it. And he was terrified all the time we'd have a baby. Huh, I said to him once, you couldn't make anyone pregnant if you wanted, it's so tiny. I didn't want to be mean to him or anything, but he made me so cross.'

'Why did you stay with him so long?'

'I don't know. It didn't seem a long time. What happened first was he took advantage of me - I hardly knew him at the time - and then I was ashamed and tried to pretend it meant something more to him than a mere sex affair, something real you know? I convinced myself he loved me like I loved him. Maybe he did, I don't know.

But he didn't know how to love - men don't, do they? He was just a great big baby. And I got so sick of playing at mother: all he wanted was to be mothered, to be spoiled like a child. And I wasn't old enough then to handle the responsibility. Trouble was I let him know me too well, let him know I worshipped him. That way I made myself vulnerable. He used to play at making me jealous. And I'd go about with something like six inches of steel in my breast. If you were ever jealous you'd know how I hurt. But you haven't, have you? Been jealous I mean. If I could only have played it cool with him, like I did at school. But I couldn't. I cared too much.'

'But you like singing?'

'Yeah, I like singing. It's the only thing I can do anyway. Really well I mean. I don't know that I won't opt out soon as I can though - all that goes with it I think. It's the pressure put on you gets me about show business. Always they're getting at you to do something you don't want to do. It's one big drag, the whole thing. And all those people one meets: one big drag. And it's not a good thing, the folk boom. It means that, in most cases, you're playing an altogether wrong kind of audience. It isn't that they don't like you or anything, or even that you can't get through to them if you work hard enough. The thing is, they're too sophisticated. It makes for a kind of barrier - do you know what I mean? You're playing a concert hall audience, and that's about as removed as you can get from the real folk thing. Like, back in the old days, a folksinger was a sort of walking newspaper. I mean, he told about what was happening. And no less truthfully than the newspapers today. But, if not the concert hall sort, you're playing a bunch of long-haired hippies who don't know what you're getting at anyway. Either way, what it means is you have to go commercial. And it's a kind of death once you make the charts: not so much that you have to change your style or anything, but that you have to submit to the machinery. Suddenly you're a star: the way it works when you're a star is while you're available to a minority, at a price, then you're okay. When you're available to a majority, at half that price, you're slipping. No one wants to know. You've been around too long. But I don't aim to do things their way too much. You get fed up singing jingle jangle songs and doing gigs around the country. Last year, I did one night stands all over the country and that's something I'll never do again. Not for anyone. There's no time to wonder, no time to lie in the grass and dream. One loses so much: one just isn't a real person any more. It's all a terrible rush and tear. One town to another, on the road all the time. Or up in the air. And I hate flying. But all these new places: you see nothing of them. Only hotel rooms, and being held up in traffic jams, and lights burning in your eyes, and a crowd of faces out there in front, and stuffy dressing-rooms with a mob beating on the door. And the same everywhere you go, no matter where it is. I have to creep away sometimes, or defy them straight out, or I'd go silly. It makes you think, the sound of your own voice that many times bigger than it actually is. Singing in a hall - or in the open, it doesn't matter which - your voice can be made to reach way beyond what it ever could without a mike. But not real at all: just an illusion. And the illusion can work on you, can make you think you're the greatest. You can get like that without knowing it even. One loves and hates it I guess. The big thing is to know when to stop, to throw it all in. I keep promising myself I'll not do another tour after this: this will be the last. But I have all these people at my heels, and breathing down my neck, and so it goes on.'

'But what would you do if you gave it up?'

'Lie in the grass and dream.' She laughed suddenly: that altogether disarming smile. A lot of white teeth. 'After I left Frankie I went to some people who have this big old place right away from it all: it's falling all in ruin and the donkey sleeps in the best bed. I slept in the kitchen on a kind of divan, and all the cats and dogs too. I was very happy there. For a meal, we didn't used to bother with plates and things. We ate out a saucepan, or out our hands. I did exactly as I liked for a while.'

'What happened?'

'Well I was getting more and more work and I started all this travelling, so I had to leave.'

'Perhaps you could get something like it yourself some time?'

'Maybe.'

There was another silence. She couldn't decide whether or not to mention marriage, but made up her mind at last.

'You should get married.' But something awkward in the way it came out: not quite as she'd intended. A little too positive, where she'd intended a suggestion only.

'Married? I don't know. All they do is fight: you see it all the time. I sometimes think I'd like to marry and especially to have a child. Or two. But I don't know about marriage. I'm afraid of it really. I think of marriage and I think of violence, and you can't bring kids up in an atmosphere like that.'

She shrugged gently. She didn't altogether see her

point of view, but there it was.

'All men aren't the same of course. I'm lucky perhaps: Anthony is one of the kindest, most considerate men one could wish to meet.'

But Miss Kumar was very reserved suddenly, non-committal.

'Yeah, I guess so. Like you said, they're around. I wonder,' she added, 'do you have the right time? Mine's stopped.'

She looked at the little gold watch Anthony had given her one birthday. Miss Kumar wore a man's watch, and with the face on the inside of her wrist. Everything about her was interesting, different. She'd begun to be very intrigued. No: she'd been, she suddenly realised, intrigued from the first. Altogether extraordinary.

'Nine o'clock,' she said. 'Are you meeting someone?'

'No.' She laughed again. 'No, I'm supposed to be in bed. As you know, we've this recording session tomorrow morning. They're such bloody awful affairs. One is allowed only a certain period of time and everyone plans to start early but no one does and then it's all panic and you're never satisfied you've done your best. A chapter of accidents: leastways, mine are. What about you? Do you have to do anything?'

'I rang Anthony at the school, said I'd be a bit late. But I suppose I ought to make a move too.'

'Could I drive you back? It doesn't make any difference.'
'Thank you.'

The evening was cold still, and wet, but not actually raining now. But reflected lights in the surface of the street and, across, the wet branches of the trees. It was very quiet. Only, distantly, London's incessant grumble.

Together with Miss Kumar, she crossed the street. Their steps rang out distinctly. Here was the car, parked at the pavement's edge. And there the railings, and beyond them the trees. There wasn't much room in the car, and very low. It was almost like sitting on the road. Through the dabble of raindrops on the windscreen she saw the curve of the long bonnet. And, over on the right, the lights of the restaurant they'd just left. The night was black, sharp and shiny. And yet a kind of softness in the air, and that glow in the sky which was London all alight and reflected in the atmosphere. She was suddenly very happy: she loved it so, London.

Miss Kumar opened the door on her side, ducked into the driving seat. She had on this black Dannimac coat - which was somehow an extension of her feeling just now about the night. About it being dark and palpable. She had to look at the coat again before she knew what she was looking at. There was a short silence while Miss Kumar got herself comfortable in her seat. Her hair fanned out in strands across the shoulders of the coat. But what was it?, she wondered, taking another look at her. What was it about her made one feel one was in the company of both a man and a woman? Simultaneously. Or alternately. There was, when she was tired, or slightly drunk, a something in her face: an oval angularity, almost a virility, and her eyes spoke very much as a man's did. They were rather bright just now, and tired, and she kept blinking as though she couldn't get the hang of anything. But then it would all change suddenly and there was a softness, almost a sweetness - those qualities a man looked for. She glanced suddenly at her hands, which had got hold of the wooden rim wheel. She'd another ring on tonight, besides the gold one. A large ring with a red stone. (Had it anything to do with her sense of the Hoffmanesque earlier on? Bright jewels into candle wax?) And, showing below the poplin texture of the coat sleeves, the fussy cuffs of the blouse she wore. They gave the hands a distinctly eighteenth-century look, showed off their peculiarly boyish build. The long, strong fingers: the squarish wrists. The light, coming through the window on that side, showed on them and partly on her face. Otherwise, it was dark. She could smell leather and engine warmth, and those other subtle odours peculiar to an expensive car. One of the hands moved down suddenly, fumbled with the ignition. But nothing happened. She didn't switch on. Instead she turned to look at her, pushed her arm out along the back of the seat.

Expecting the engine to come to life, and then nothing happening, the silence was like a blow on the head. All Knightsbridge listened she thought. Why on earth didn't she say something, this girl in the black coat with her eighteenth-century hands and her tired eyes? Rather like a dream. That extreme eroticism she'd often experienced in dreams but never in waking. Not for years anyway. It was, she supposed, a proposal. All she saw of her was the gleam of her strong, regular teeth which seemed to have forced her mouth partly open. Other than that she was just a silhouette, a dream. In which case, what difference did it make?

She half turned in her seat, put out her hand and took hold of the girl's face. It was quite a shock, the real feeling of her. Warm, rather coarse skin. Flesh and blood. And what touch meant when one was unable to see! And, moving her fingers further in, the rather more secret warmth of her scalp, the springing roots of her hair. The flames engulfed her - or was it the candlelight? - and the thick, sweet burning incense. (It must have had some sort of perfume, the candle. She'd pinched it out before they left and the smell of the liquid wax was like hyacinths.) Tentatively, Miss Kumar touched her lips with her own. She felt the gentle pressure of the firm, malleable mouth, was confused as to her own reactions. But before she could make up her mind the girl pulled away suddenly, gulping like an adolescent, and stared out through the windscreen.

'What is it? What's the matter?'

But she only gulped again, then threw her arm across the steering wheel and burst into tears.

She made to take her into her arms but she resisted hung on to the wheel and kept her face hidden. She sat back, waited. She could smell, in the enclosed space, the wine on the girls breath: her skin, too, exuded an odour of alcohol. She wondered, briefly, why she put up with her. But knew, while the thought was still in her head. With herself, it was so much more than a physical thing.

'Sarah?'

No reply. She reached out, took hold of a strand of her hair.

'What you want is a good night's sleep. Go straight back to the hotel and get into bed. Don't worry about me: I'll get a taxi.'

She snuffed and sniffed a minute or two more, then dashed the tears away with the back of her hand.

'I'm sorry. I don't know what's the matter with me: I'm not unhappy at all.'

Was she, or wasn't she? She didn't know, couldn't

fathom it just yet.

'No, I know.' She took hold of her face again, turned it towards her. 'Too much to drink, that's all.'

A sudden glare of defiance - something she hadn't seen before.

'No.'

'Yes.' Smiling, but firm. She waited a moment, but the girl said nothing. 'Do you know this has happened each time I've seen you? You were tight last night, and more than tight the night before. Why?'

She looked out through the windscreen and seemed to think it over a minute. She'd that lost nightmare look about her again which worried her so, alarmed her even.

'I can't explain,' she said at last. 'I'm not hooked or anything like that. I don't have to have it.' And, turning again: 'You believe me don't you?'

'Is that what you believe?'

'I don't understand.' That fricative sound again on the S, and her speech thick as though her tongue got in the way.

'Never mind now. Another time.' Not impatient with her exactly, just a little tired.

'No, don't be like that. I haven't offended you, have I?'

She looked steadily at the girl.

'If you'd told me you didn't understand two, three days ago, I think I should have been offended. Moreover, I'd not have bothered with you again. As it is, we'll forget all about it.'

Both were silent a while. The girl got out her handkerchief and blew her nose.

'When can I see you? Where?' - pulling herself together with an effort. 'I don't have to be anywhere tomorrow afternoon - not as far as I know.'

Yes, complications, Awkward really. Anthony, of course, would be at the school. But she abhorred deception, was never comfortable practising it.

'When do you think your session, or whatever you call it, will be over?'

'I don't know. Lunchtime I hope.'

'Would you like to come to my place? And then we could think of something.'

'Yes. But your husband?'

'He'll be at the school.' So it began all over again, another small deception. But no: not the same. Not a bit the same. She'd never given them a second thought, her previous infidelities. (What were they anyway? Glorified flirtations, nothing more.) Anthony had his amours: she had hers. But they'd meant nothing to her, those few young men. (What was it, Anthony had once wanted to know, about young men? Why these dreadful boys? And it was true. They came like pins to a magnet, goodness only knows why. Young women too. And she must play the lover, or mother, or both. A role she accepted as perfectly natural: she loved to pet, to comfort - needed to in fact. And so they came. Sought her protection, she supposed, more than anything.)

'All right. I'll be there about two, or maybe just before.'

'You will remember?'

'Yes. Are you sure I can't drive you home?'

'No, don't bother. You need some sleep.' She searched for the door handle. 'How does it work, this thing?'

'No, that's the window. Pardon me.'

She reached across, unfastened the door. The slight pressure of her body as she leaned across made her feel

61

again as she had when they'd kissed. But it was too much: she was tired. And something wrong. Not that they'd kissed, the kiss rather. It had asked too much of her, sapped her somehow. She no longer needed this physical aspect of a relationship.

'There you are.'

'Thank you.'

She got out quickly, banged the door, waited. The car moved off: she waved. A small, awkward gesture - she couldn't think why. Perhaps because now, standing here on the wet pavement, what had happened between them didn't seem possible. And then, with a sense of something snapped off, unfulfilled, she hurried along the street in search of a taxi.

JANE

It had got quite dark in the room. Only the firelight jumping on the walls and ceiling. She'd lit the fire because it was so cold, though she'd thought she'd finished with them this year. Outside, it still rained. Lying against her, Sarah laughed suddenly.

'So English, the weather. I can't believe it was so hot a couple of days ago.'

'No, it doesn't seem possible.'

'This room is so like you,' she went on after a minute. No longer laughing, but with her face pressed into her shoulder and speaking in a sort of mumbling monotone with her eyes closed. There were dark shadows under her eyes, as though someone had pressed into the flesh with the side of his thumb. (Something she'd seen Anthony do time out of number, working on a portrait head - on anything, working with his thumb. Probing, scoring, flattening.) 'Quiet. And balanced. Like you're the axis on which the room is slowly turning. It makes sense somehow.'

She smiled a little, but said nothing. But pressed the girl's face against her, smoothed it reassuringly. With her hand over her eyes, the fingers spread a little, as though to guard them from the light.

'I've always wanted to know someone like you. I've been looking so hard for you I can't believe I found you at last. Literally looking into people's faces. You've no idea how different I feel with you. Away from it, from everything. You're not like all the other people I know. You made everything good for me yesterday after that affair in the Square.' She lifted her head suddenly, caressed the shoulder she'd been lying on. Passed her hand over it with a tentative, fumbling motion. 'I get so scared sometimes. Scared of everything, and myself too. The way I react, I think. I mean, I could have killed somebody yesterday. No I couldn't, but it was that sort of feeling. It scares me to think I have it in me to feel like that. It means I'm no better than them really and I haven't got any right to stand up and talk about people killing each other in Vietnam, or anywhere. That's what's so wrong, don't you think? There's nobody good, no really good people.'

She looked down, saw the open shirt and the white gash of the brassiere against the smooth textured skin of the girl's body. A sallow, olive colour. And dusky where the forms changed direction, were shadowed. Very small but perfect breasts. And, because of the way she sat, half sprawled, the projection of the rib cage on one side. And then the neat navel. But the nakedness cut off suddenly by the dark blue of the jeans she wore. Rather slim hips.

'Come along, button this up.'

'Why?'

She didn't answer at once, reached for a small medallion she saw around her neck.

'What's this?'

'Oh,' looking down at it, 'something called a miraculous medal. Did you never hear of it?'

'No.'

'The Virgin Mary. I've had it since I was at school.' She thought a minute. 'I have this thing about her: she must have been a wonderful person, don't you think? I see her as someone who had this definite beauty thing going for her, spiritual beauty I mean. I don't know if she was a virgin or not: I don't think it matters. I think she must have kept that feeling about her even if she wasn't.'

'I haven't really thought about it.'

'I figure she looks after me pretty good anyhow.'

She let the medallion fall, began to button the girl's blouse.

'What I was going to say was do you know what time it is?'

'No. I don't want to.' And pulled away, smiling. 'Lady with the black gloves. I know because you left them when you left your handbag.'

'You didn't go through my handbag?'

'Yes, because I wanted to know all about you. And the gloves said everything. You made me think of Anna Karenina. But before I found the gloves: when I first saw you, sitting on that chair. But maybe not. She was so cruel, Anna Karenina. Not a nice person at all, and I hate immoral women. Just the gloves I guess.' There was a sudden small explosion in the fire, a hiss of escaping air. The room was darker, then the flames leapt again. 'You know, I'd do anything for you. Anything at all. That's what's so beautiful about you: you make me aware of the unimportance of everything else. I'd be your slave if you wanted. Yes I would,' she said. Fiercely, through her teeth, and dug her fingernails into her. 'You could have me on a collar and chain and I'd walk on all fours.' She took up a handful of her own long hair, touched it softly against her face. 'I'd wash your feet with my tears, and dry them with my hair. Why don't you make me? Why don't you beat me, and bruise me, and make me?'

'My darling Sarah, do get off me. I've pins and needles in my arm'.

'Okay, okay.' And, laughing a little, sat back in the other corner of the sofa and reached for the flat tin of small cigars that was on the coffee table. (Behind which loomed the tall iron candlestand Anthony had picked up in the Portobello Road.) 'So prosaic, so English.'

'Perhaps.'

'Not perhaps. Definitely. But not the teapot piddling away into a dainty cup - not that kind of English.'

Some of the things she came out with shocked her a little, and yet were acceptable because she was so absolutely frank. One couldn't possibly be cross with her. Smiling, she reached for one of her hands.

'Magpie.'

'Why?'

'Because of all these rings and things. Do you like jewellery?'

'Yes, but not too elaborate. And it has to be good. No garbage, you know?' She hesitated before lighting the cigar, looked intently at her. 'If you persist in being prosaic I'll jump on you and tear you with my claws.'

'A moment ago you were my slave.'

She blew smoke out through her nostrils, crossed her legs one over the other and looked at her bare foot.

'Yeah, that was a moment ago.'

'Oh, I see.' And was reminded for the umpteenth time today of how she'd seen her in the restaurant last night, as a debauched young goddess. She looked a bit like that now.

The girl questioned with her eyebrows. 'What?'

'I said I see.'

She let go her hand, took all the hair back from her face. The firelight was red on the high structure of the nose, the bones of the face. Gently, she touched her cheek. Somewhere, the cigar smouldered. She could smell it, saw the tremulous haze of smoke. And then the girl looked away, looked at the floor. Invitation: capitulation.

And at the same time that odd modesty, as though till now she'd submitted to no one. But, suddenly careful, she sat back from her a little. The girl looked quickly at her, hesitated. And then, all in a hurry, reached down her hand and opened her trousers and slipped her arms around her, drew her down, begged her in whispers to make love with her, and she could feel the clawing movement of her hands across her shoulders, over her back. She was shocked as she'd never been in intercourse with Anthony, was terribly aware of the bare, bony foot which caressed her thigh with female voracity. But then, sensing a resentment of her timidity, she allowed the girl to take her hand, to touch it against the rough pubic hair, to reveal the secrets lodged there. And felt the spasmodic muscular response. Felt too, but with a sense of not fully participating (there was of course this difference in their ages: she herself no longer required sensation), the reciprocal action of the girl's fingernails on her back. She was terribly afraid suddenly of this aspect of their relationship. She doubted she could give her the satisfaction she wanted, doubted her abilities in this direction. She was afraid she'd disappoint her, spoil the whole thing. And the male role was strange to her: she'd not the smallest understanding of it.

She needn't have been afraid, she realised after. It seemed the sex business was incidental, or at any rate secondary. She wasn't sure really. But what the girl seemed to want more than anything was the disinterested protection she was able, as a woman, to offer her. She kissed her many times, and said she was like a mother to her, only more, and she loved her more than she could have thought possible. And took hold suddenly of her hand and pressed it to her face, and then to her lips, and said thank you several times, thanking and kissing alternately.

At last she got up and, watching her still, straightened her clothes.

'I'd like to play something for you - I brought the guitar specially.'

'Thank you. How did your session go by the way?'

'Pretty well. First time they kept getting too much of my hand and body movements because they'd put a mike on the instrument. Second time we took it off. They thought maybe the guitar was a bit quiet then, but

I think it's mostly recorded too loud anyway. It sounded to me like a good compromise so we called it a day. Time was running out anyway. But some of the tracks on the last album I did, the guitar was right forward. That's all right for the intro, but then the voice should take over. This was just a single I cut this morning though. I don't agree really, but Cassidi thinks I ought to put out more singles here. I keep telling him that market's the wrong one for me: I shan't last with the kids over here anyway. They're not really with the folk thing: it's just a fad.' She shrugged, smiled. 'Still, it's them that's making me a living right now. Wait here, won't you? I'll go get my instrument. I've got it in the back of the car.'

'Will you come to the concert I'm playing Wednesday?' she asked when she got back. 'I could let you have a couple of tickets.'

'Oddly enough Anthony brought two home yesterday. One of the students at the school: he wasn't able to go after all, put his tickets up for sale.'

'That's great. I'd like you to be there.' Suddenly serious, she played across the strings. 'You know,' she said, but not looking up, 'Wednesday is the day after tomorrow.'

'Yes.' And what after? No, she couldn't think about it. 'It doesn't make sense, does it? I mean, I've only just met you.'

'What are you going to play?'

She didn't answer at once. Then:

'Well I thought I'd play you this. I arranged it myself once when I didn't have anything to do, because it wasn't actually written for plectrum guitar.'

A rather sad little piece. Spanish perhaps? The melody rose and fell, but softly. She played rather well: a great deal better than she'd expected, considering she mostly used the instrument for accompaniment only. And, while she played, seemed to cut herself off somehow. One had an impression of total involvement: a lot to do with the way she sat, the instrument across her thigh, hugged to her, and that complete absorption with what she was doing. It was almost frightening. But not frightening, no. It moved her rather. But then, when she'd finished playing, she was laughing again. A complete change of mood. Or she was shamming perhaps? - it was hard to tell.

'You know, show business is the weirdest thing. I didn't tell you about what happened last year, when I was going to pay my first visit here. My manager said to me look Sarah, your image is all wrong. It's not exciting enough. They see you over there as a bit of a - you read me? Let them see you, the Press, and tell them you're a nymphomaniac and a dipsomaniac, and a this and a that - whatever you like. But that you're just an ordinary girl at heart, and all you really want is a home and family just like any other girl. The kids over there, they really swing y'know. They'd buy that. So I said shit my image and what you said to me to say is all a contradiction anyway. I can't go tell them I'm a nymphomaniac and a dipsomaniac and then make them believe I'm just an ordinary girl at heart. So he said, so all right, it's a contradiction: it'll give 'em something to think about. You can't beat them you see, so I met the Press and I said to them yes I'm a dipsomaniac and a junkie and I've slept about and I've been in prison and I once wanted to be a nun and I saw Jesus Christ sitting on the dustbin in the back yard and I'm just an ordinary girl at heart. Biggest laugh of all was they took it for bloody gospel and printed every word.'

'Oh they're like that, the newspapers. I suppose he has a big say in your affairs, your manager?'

'More or less, yeah. I mean, we spend a hell of a lot of time together. Trouble with those guys is they don't know where to stop: I have to keep reminding him my private life is my own affair or he'd have me on a ball and chain, talking out through his mouth. I'd never go tell the newspapers that kind of story again - or any kind of story - not for anything. Jesus, I hate to think about it. I suppose, though, we don't get on too badly. In a sense I respect him because he's never tried anything, never made a pass at me I mean. He doesn't seem to have any kind of sex life at all come to think of it: maybe he's too old now. All he cares about is money. So okay. What I don't like is that the whole thing - my relationship with him - is founded on duplicity. He says yes to them and no to me. Or no to them and yes to me. It's all a compromise, doesn't get you anywhere. Except, maybe, where they want you to be. That's what gets me: you have to fight all the time if you want to feel you're a person at all, and not just a piece of property. And I hate untruths, I hate duplicity. The whole thing stinks, you know?'

'Yes. I know.'

'Worst of all, it can rub off on you: you're acting the same way before you know it. You have to watch yourself all the time if you don't want to end up the kind of phoney creep Cassidi is. I guess, though, we all start out with good intentions.'

'Yes, I suppose so. But you love it all really? I'd imagine show business is more of a disease than an occupation?'

'I don't know. There's all kinds of aspects to it. Like I said before, one loves and hates it. I couldn't imagine myself doing anything else - any other kind of job I mean. It's the characters you have to deal with, all those creeps and phonies, gets me.' .

For the next half-hour, skilfully but quite unmaliciously, she told hilarious stories about the various types of people she'd come up against in show business. She laughed at her till her sides ached. And then begged her to play something else, to be serious again. While she played, she caught sight of her bag there in the corner of the sofa. The bag was open and there was a wallet of photos inside. She asked did she mind if she saw them?

'No.' But stopped playing suddenly. 'Only there's one there taken when I was with Frankie - maybe you'd rather not see it?'

'Nonsense.' She looked. A small, closely cropped young man in a striped shirt and jeans. Rather attractive in a boyish sort of way. A little cynical perhaps, and certainly an introvert. They'd been taken together apparently, but the other part was cut away. 'Why do you hold on to it?'

'I don't know. I never thought about it. I didn't know I still had it.'

'But you did. You just said to me there was one of you with him.'

'Well I did and I didn't if you know what I mean.'

'Yes,' she said. But not absolutely sure what she meant. There was a rather awkward silence. The girl picked at the guitar a moment, then said:

'He made me feel such an idiot, just sitting there and looking at my nakedness. He'd ask me to go undress: he was going to draw me. Then he'd sit there looking like he hated me. And all kinds of things: I can't tell you some of the things he used to make me do for him.'

She rather felt this was getting off the subject, but let it go. She looked at some of the other pictures. A smiling girl on an open veranda, leaning up against a post and half in shadow. Dusty denims, the same long hair. And three oddly assorted dogs. She was holding out something to one of the dogs: had broken a piece off something she was eating - she'd the rest of it in the other hand. It was taken, she thought, in the evening: something to do with the colour of the light. The worn knees of the denims, the pale colour of the shirt, stood out the way light colours did in the evening.

'Are these all yours, the dogs?'

She laughed suddenly:

'No. They belong to these people I stayed with. They would keep gettin' married you see. In the end they didn't know what to do with them, they'd so many. At the time that was taken they'd about six.'

'Goodness.' She examined the picture more closely. 'But what a very pretty girl.'

'Yeah. You wouldn't think, looking at that, the awful things I done in my life.'

'Darling, haven't we all sometime or other?'

'But bad things and nasty things and mean things. I don't think I've done a good thing in all my life.'

'I don't believe it. I can't imagine it.'

'But you must believe it.'

One of her forking over a bonfire (she wished she wouldn't talk like that), half screened in smoke and the flames jumping up red.

She put the pictures down suddenly, folded her arms.

'Perhaps you blame yourself for the way it worked out, that particular love affair?'

She thought a while, was reluctant perhaps to admit to any kind of guilt but didn't want to excuse herself either.

'I don't know. Maybe we were both too young at the time. I don't think we could either of us change, but I do feel like maybe it could have worked better if we'd both tried harder. I was wrong to keep paying him back: that way I laid myself open, he could keep on giving me more. Also I didn't try to understand what was the matter with him. But, like I already said, I got fed up playing at mother. I needed someone stronger. It was all a terrible strain.'

She was going to say something in reply, some casual remark, when suddenly the front door banged.

'There, you see. Anthony.'

But, remarkably calm, the girl grabbed a magazine, saw to her buttons, seated herself politely with the remains of her cigar (which had gone out a long while ago), just a second before Anthony came into the room. For herself, she switched the curtains across and inaugurated a passably intelligent conversation considering. Clothes and so on, the new short skirts. But the room suddenly so guilty she was sure Anthony would know at once all that had happened. And, good heavens!, no light. They'd forgotten the light. Who could possibly see to read a magazine in this gloom? The fire was low: had crumbled, fallen. She was aware, in the semi dark, of Anthony's surprise, his sense of intrusion. (There'd been a similar incident a year or two ago now: a young man, all rather innocent really. But Anthony had come in, found them together with the light off. And now, as she did then, she felt that the situation was in terribly bad taste. She'd have given anything for it not to have happened. It made it seem she was always at it or something dreadful like that. Promiscuous, that was how she felt.) She reached out, put on the lamp. Quite a glare after the red glow to which her eyes had got used. (And all the little familiar objects around it: the paper weight, the brass ashtray, Anthony's special cigarettes.) And Sarah, there in the corner of the sofa, her legs crossed, her back to the door, her bare feet suddenly so naked, would persist in making the most absurd faces at her while she spoke sensibly of this and that, standing here in the yellow glare of the lamp with her hands before her as though in prayer. With Anthony there at the open door, she was forced to keep a poker face while enduring an astonishing variety of facial expressions.

'Oh, I'm sorry,' Anthony apologised, 'I didn't mean to interrupt.'

He was puzzled of course, sensed something unusual. Had Sarah been a man, he'd have known at once. As it was, he was foxed because of her sex. (She couldn't imagine though how anyone could have been blind to the girl's bisexuality: any woman would have seen it at once, would have known exactly what was going on.)

'Nonsense, darling. I was just beginning to wonder where you were.'

Sarah made at putting out her cigar, got up.

'I hope you don't mind: I borrowed one of your cigars.'

'No. Not at all.'

'I'd better be off. I didn't realise it was so late.'

'Don't let me chase you away.'

She glanced quickly, rather coolly at him.

'No. I just have to go.'

'But you'll come tomorrow - to the school?'

She slung the guitar on her back, smiled briefly.

'Yes, I'd forgotten. At what time?'

'Perhaps during the afternoon classes - or just after would be better. There's no one about then. Would that be all right for you?'

'Thank you. I guess so. Good-bye, Mrs Stankovich.'

If reluctant to go she gave no sign, was perfectly collected.

'I'll see you out,' she said.

'Thank you.'

In the hall, a quick fumbling embrace made awkward because of the instrument.

'When can I see you?'

'Darling, I don't know. What are you doing tomorrow?'

'Nothing. Except to go see the art school. I wish I hadn't said I would.'

'Never mind. I'll think of something. I'll ring you first thing in the morning.'

SARAH

She was cleaning her teeth when the phone began ringing in the bedroom.

Was she too early?, Mrs Stankovich wondered. She hoped she hadn't woken her?

'No. I'm up already. What are we going to do?'

She was thinking, why didn't they drive off somewhere? Out into the country for instance. Somewhere away from everybody.

'Yeah, we'll do that. Anywhere you want. I'll pick you up, shall I?'

Yes, that would be best.

'At what time?'

Whenever she was ready.

'I'm nearly ready now. We won't plan anything, we'll just go.' She took the phone away from her ear a moment, smiled into it. Mrs Stankovich couldn't see this though, so she said: 'I just smiled at you.' And then kissed into the phone, like she did for her brother. 'But take care of yourself: be there when I come.'

(Some laughter at the other end.) She was a great big silly: of course she'd be there.

'I keep being scared it's all a dream, that's why. Well, I won't be long.'

Back in the bathroom, the phone went again. Passing the looking-glass - her hair all runched up still, she must get a rake through it - she knew something had gone wrong. It had. But not irreparably. It was Stephen, to say he was back rather suddenly (had he been somewhere?) and needed the car. Just for today. Could she bear to part with it? She could have it again tomorrow if she wished.

'Yeah, okay.'

So would it be all right if he came and collected it?

'Yes, I'll get them to bring it round. You can pick it up at the Embankment Entrance.'

Jolly good. But she was sure it was all right? She hadn't intended to use it today?

(He was so sweet, she couldn't upset him.)

'No. I can always take a taxi in any case.'

Yeah. Well. That buggered things up a bit. She wondered whether or not to ring Mrs Stankovich but, reaching for the phone, thought it wasn't really necessary. She'd take a taxi, and they'd change their plans accordingly.

She took her hand off the receiver and, like it was a signal she'd given, the damn thing began ringing all over again. It was daddy Cassidi, calling from his suite. (She could just imagine him sitting up in bed with his breakfast tray, his newspapers - *New York Herald Tribune, Time magazine*, the *Daily Express* - and silk pyjamas. The jacket open and all that shapeless, fallen flesh speckled like a fish in the bright morning light, and his navel sagging over the loose trousers.) Very suave, rather distant. Like he was when he was annoyed about something.

Where was she all yesterday?

(She smiled a little.)

'You mean during the afternoon? In wonderland. No, but seriously, I said I wouldn't be in - do you remember?'

No, he didn't remember.

'Yeah, lunchtime. I said to you. I said there were one or two things I wanted to get: I'm crazy about the shops over here.'

And he'd said not to be out, remember? (Some mirthless haw-hawing at the other end.) No: he just wished she wouldn't run about on her own, that's all. He'd been going to take her to the Scotch of St James's during the evening incognito of course - for a quiet drink. Where was she then?

(But she hated the way he used stupid words like incognito.)

'Well, like I went to bed early. Leastways, comparatively. First we were at Dolly's-'

We?

'Yes. You remember that disc jockey guy, Sammy Someone-Or-Other? Well he rang me and said would I like to go to Dolly's, and I said fine, so he picked me up here at the hotel.'

When was this? Why hadn't she said?

(She examined her fingernails.)

'I looked in but you were asleep. I didn't bother waking you, you looked so pretty.'

(A pause.)

What time did she get back? He rang her room at about eleven.

'I don't know. About one I think. I had some friends here. Well, some people - you know? Two of The What's Their Names, and a guy I've never seen before who said he met me in Illinois and that he was a soul singer, and that girl who's got a hit right now with a Jack Schuler song. I can't even remember her name - Sweetheart was it? Darling? Yeah, Grace Darling or something. Anyhow, we had quite a ball. I don't know what happened to Silver: we left him at Dolly's. The What's Their Names brought their instruments along - one of them has an autoharp - and we all played together. What happened to you? Why didn't you come on in and join us?'

That time of night, he was fast asleep. He went to bed after he rang her room. Did she see a newspaper yesterday? - he'd forgot to ask in the morning. A lot of bad publicity over that Square affair. And they had the name of her hotel - goodness knows how they'd got hold of that. He thought she hadn't wanted anyone to know where she'd be staying, that they were keeping it quiet this time?

'But I didn't tell anybody.'

Well, there it was. In the paper.

'Don't bother, I'm not putting my nose outside today. They sure are looking after us here: I've got all I want and more.' She laughed. 'The bell hop just showed me pictures of his sister's wedding, and lent me his transistor radio. I didn't like to say I didn't need it. And the chambermaid is half through telling me her life story. She's an Italian, and writes back home every night before she says her prayers.'

Yes. Well, how was she?

'Mending, thanks. If you mean about last night.'

(He ignored this.)

But now the thing was, and this my dear was why he'd rung actually, could she go to Portland House today?

(Clickety-click: she'd heard it coming. She knew there was something.)

'I don't get it.'

Portland House. To tie in with her visit, the company had run a competition for the best window display. The retail side. And she was giving the prizes. Sammy S. Silver, he'd be there too. They'd rung him here at the hotel and he'd said he thought she would - she would of course?

'But hell, I don't need that kind of publicity.'

There was no publicity attached: one of the trade papers would be there, that was all. It was to be a completely private affair. And rather a nice surprise for the winners if she went.

'I'm sorry. I can't do it.'

Had she something else today? The company, after all, had put a lot of time and money into the campaign. (So whose fault was that?) It all added up to bigger sales on her records. They knew what a good girl she was, were relying on her generosity.

'So?'

Then she must ring them herself, tell them she couldn't make it after all.

(Desperately disappointed, she thought it over a minute.)

'What time? How long for?'

Eleven-thirty. An hour at the most.

'But they can't expect me to take on an engagement out of the blue. I wouldn't do it for the President even, not that kind of stunt I wouldn't.'

But, honey, they hadn't expected anything. It was up to her entirely. Sammy S. Silver would deputise as originally planned if she didn't want to do it. If she did, they'd do it together. But she must ring them herself.

'All right, since you fixed it. But I bloody wish you hadn't.'

Good. He'd ring them back at once - or she could if she preferred.

'No, you.' (What did he think he was here for?)

'Good, good.'

He rang off. She looked at the phone a minute, then got herself a line.

'I want to speak to Mrs Stankovich. Thank you. Hello? Yeah. The lousiest thing you could think of. Cassidi just rang me: I have to hand out some prizes at Portland House. What? No, my recording company here. They ran a competition or something. Eleven-thirty. Oh I don't know, it doesn't matter anyway. What can we do? - that's what I'm wondering. You know I arranged to meet your husband at the school this afternoon - can't I get out of that somehow?'

No, she didn't think she ought. He'd begin to think she was keeping her all to herself. But Anthony was having dinner with friends: she'd said she'd rather not go, so he was going alone. So what about dinner somewhere? Or at her place even?

'But that's hours away. What do I do till then - in between times I mean?'

There must be something she had to do?

'But I want to be with you. It seems such a waste. Tomorrow will be pretty hopeless, and I'm off again next morning.'

What was to happen then? What could be arranged?

'Lunch. We could have lunch. And then do something, anything. Can't you think of something?'

They'd have lunch then. And think of something after. Could she meet her at Gow's at about one or just before?

'Where's that?'

St Martin's Lane - not far from the art school actually. Just around the corner from William IV Street.

'Yes, I'll see you there. But be there, won't you?'

Yes, of course she would. Not to be a silly billy.

(She relaxed a little, smiled.)

'Watch out for me because I'll be in dark glasses and a false beard.'

If with the latter, she'd look most devastatingly handsome she was sure. She'd rather she didn't though - suppose it came unstuck?

(She laughed out loud. Things weren't so black after all.)

'But be there, won't you?'

One hour later Cassidi called the desk, asked them to get him a cab. Yeah, the main entrance would do. And - talking over his shoulder at her - if there was anyone waiting, all the better. Today he could begin showing her off: she wasn't a secret any longer.

And, leaving the hotel, across the street they were building or repairing something. Up that narrow lane:

a tower of ugly scaffolding. And, in the street, all bright sunlight that bounced back off the running stream of vehicles, glared and glittered.

The cab came in under the cold shade of the forecourt and one of those guys in uniform went quickly forward, snatched open the door while the cab still rolled. A few pigeons went suddenly and awkwardly up into the air.

But, unexpected, an assorted mob all come to gawp. And press men pushing for pictures. (She didn't really believe, when Cassidi said about it, anyone would wait around this time of day just to see her. Maybe he'd called the Press, said what time they'd be leaving. He got a big kick out of this kind of thing, loved all the publicity.) She wanted to turn around and go right back in but Cassidi was holding on to her arm and she'd have hated herself for it anyway. Instead, she put her head down and made a dash for it. The grey tarmacadam and the cold shadow and pigeons scattering like scared hens. And coming down again all soft like snow, and the soft flutter of their wings. The uniformed guy still had the cab, but they were cut off from him suddenly by the eager surge of the crowd. (Crowds on a small scale scared her more than thousands.) They were all putting their faces over each other's shoulders and grinning and either a bit self-conscious or too familiar. They mostly wanted just to look: some wanted autographs. But this, if she was honest, was when she liked people least. Maybe because they took such liberties one didn't feel human at all, but like God knows what. Hands, all wriggling and prehensile and grasping and demanding, caught at her clothes and person. Notebooks and pencils were pushed into her face. Smiling all the same - it came automatically, didn't mean anything- she ducked the waving books and pencils, ducked the anonymous greedy hands that reached to caress her hair. Someone, right the back, said ah fuck. Just to show her. And she smiled at him too, though something inside said hell and felt the injustice like a small physical pain. Like when you're in a tearing hurry and you knock yourself on something and you're too bothered just then to understand how much it hurt. And all shouted broken sentences: press men trying to keep her from getting away and wanting answers to their questions. How long had she been here? Why had she kept her arrival a secret? And what about the march: whose idea was that? Did she feel the march was successful or not? Had she done any shopping yet? Did she mean to stay on after the concert? - he'd heard she'd like to stay on a while. She just smiled, waved them off. But Cassidi stopped, said a few words to them. She was half aware someone had cut a button off her sleeve and another had got tight hold of her hand like she'd never let it go. More girls than boys, and all looking a bit like herself. And what about Vietnam?, the press men wanted to know. What was her real feeling about American policy in Vietnam? Stressing the 'real' like she hadn't made it clear yet. Still smiling, she shook her head. And ducked into the cab at last, and Cassidi came tumbling after. The door banged shut on them and the vehicle was waved off. For a second or two it was semi dark, and yellow shapes moved in front of her eyes like when you've been looking at the sun. And then they turned off into the stream of traffic and she could see again and, huddled back in the shadow of the darkened rear window, as far away from Cassidi as she could get because she didn't want him to start talking, found that though she was warm her teeth were chattering and all her body was hunched and tense. Her head had begun to ache: she closed her eyes till it swam more slowly, came to a standstill at last. More or less.

And then out of the cab again and the sun burning down on her head a minute and then into the cool, efficient building and down some stairs and some more stairs. A plain, austere handrail, like in a block of flats, and their steps echoed like someone was after them still. And then when they'd got themselves tidied up - a small safety pin was found for the cuff that had lost its button - a large rectangular room plushly carpeted and smelling of hi fi equipment and sherry and hot lights and cigar smoke. And that disc jockey guy creating awkward laughs, playing the fool in a frenzied effort to get the whole thing going. She was introduced to a middle-aged, middle-class woman in a wild hat. She'd a thin, very red mouth and laughed a lot in a nervous sort of way - screamed out loud when they sprung the genuine article on her. And there was a fair, pale, pop-eyed girl in a dolly-rocker dress who looked like she was scared to death and said nothing at all. (Suddenly and completely cut off from the sun and sky, her head began to go round again.) And company publicity and display material all over the place: and all this crap she was talking, and the sales manager's big happy laugh, and the wine in her glass, and Cassidi's crummy jokes and his I Am God attitude to these small, harmless people. And feeling one moment that she was still in the cab, the next that she hadn't yet left her room back at the hotel. And, everywhere she looked, her own big smile faltered back at her. There was a display all along one wall: sleeves of her LPs, publicity blow ups, one enormous profile in black and white singing into a mike, and her name in all kinds of sizes - but who the hell was Sarah Kumar? This yakkety-yak female who was doing her best to convince two complete strangers she was quite ordinary really, just like them, didn't bite anyhow? All she knew was she hated every stupid minute of it, couldn't think what had made her agree to it. (She kept seeing, inside her head, the way the thin-lipped woman had looked when they said to her who she was. The way she'd screamed and the way her hand flew to her mouth like she was choking or something. I've got all your records, she kept saying. Over and over, like - yeah, like a record that had got stuck and playing at the wrong speed too, and like she didn't know what she was saying anyway. And those circular lights, sunk in the ceiling, kept flashing on her glasses like an SOS.) There was a low platform at one end of the room - maybe they gave disc recitals here? - and on the platform a table, and something on the table. A phonograph she thought, or a tape recorder. The prize anyhow. But Gow's - that was what she hung on to. A place called Gow's in the St Martin's Lane. She hung on to it like to a rope over a precipice. But did she know anyone called Stankovich? She'd dreamed it maybe? If I am dreaming let me not - what was that crappy old song? (Yeah, there were things she didn't like too.) But when was all this going to end? When would she get away from here? From the smiles all over the wall that got more and more fixed and glassy so that she thought all those mouths would give up suddenly, would snap shut. Like her own did at last. She'd never been so bored. For God's sake Cassidi, get her out of here.

SARAH

She went back to the hotel first and changed out of
the cotton dress into jeans, a denim shirt with a button-
down collar, and next-to-nothing sandals. Yeah, and she
needed the shades. The big, thick-framed ones that gave
her this insect look, changed her whole aspect somehow.
The phone rang but she ignored it. She was scared if she
picked it up it'd be something that'd keep her.

So then a Pan Am bag with a few odds and ends, some
English money and that, and then walked out the back way
like any old body and got a cab along the Embankment.

She paid the cab off in the cramped little street - cars
parked all along the sidewalk - and pushed a funny
old door and found herself in the small, crowded bar.
Except herself, they were all men. Men in dark suits and
bowler hats. The light wasn't very good though the sun
shone through the corner window, warmed a section
of red leather seat. But she didn't take the glasses off,
and at first got impressions through her nose only. And
a dark sense of atmosphere, warm and tangible like a
big person pushing against her. There was a smell of
beer and spirits and cigarette smoke. And food too. And
somewhere inside her head she saw table napkins and
cruets and cutlery because the smell of the place made
her think of these things at once. She even saw the fine,
yellowy dust on the polished blunt nose of the pepper
pot. All in an instant, a flash. But then, as her eyes got
more used to being inside, saw that there were tables
and chairs and a hat-stand and a way through to the
restaurant and a white-faced clock right over it that had
that weighty, lunchtime look about it. Later, when the

place had emptied and all the little men in bowler hats had gone, it would ease up somehow, relax, get into a reflective sort of mood again. There'd be no one to check his watch off against it, to keep darting it quick glances through the tobacco haze, the beer smell, the energetic jumble of conversation.

One or two looked curiously at her - because of the way she was dressed she thought, they were all so conservative. But Mrs Stankovich wasn't there. A waiter came to her, doubted her business maybe? Said could he help madam, and she had to explain she was waiting for somebody. She'd like a drink perhaps? Yes she'd drink a large whisky - and sat at a small table near the door. The door kept opening and shutting, but strange faces every time. Then she thought to take a look at the clock, and saw she was early by ten minutes or so. Right on the stroke of one Mrs Stankovich came quickly in looking harassed and vague in that way English women did - and it was like everything changed, the whole atmosphere of the place. Everybody seemed a bit more interesting and she'd have done anything for them, these men in dark suits and smelling of beer and talking loudly, importantly, in pairs or groups or reading their newspapers in the light of the window. With the falling away of anxiety, she loved them all.

They went together into the restaurant and there were white cloths, complicated arrangements of cutlery, a discreet lighting of sorts - she didn't notice what exactly. Mrs Stankovich had booked a table: the waiter showed them to it. They ate fish, and drank a glass of white wine. The room got crowded. All around, people came and went. Mrs Stankovich drank black coffee, she drank brandy.

(Several brandies. And saw Mrs Stankovich look funny
at her when she held on to the glass with both hands like
she was scared she'd drop it. Her hand shook sometimes,
she didn't know why. It just happened. Maybe, after all
- no, she didn't want to think about it.) And smoked a
cigar. And, half turned in Mrs Stankovich's direction (they
sat side by side), looked hard at her to be sure this was
actually happening. But still she couldn't make it seem
real: it was like a dream. And then, in the middle of some
nonsense she was talking, Mrs Stankovich told her off for
looking so pointedly at her and she laughed and then
tried hard to be serious and then laughed again. How did
she know she was looking pointedly at her? How could
she see with the glasses on? The glasses, Mrs Stankovich
said, made no difference. And to behave herself please,
and face the other way. No, she wouldn't. She couldn't
afford to lose one minute of her.

'I've something to tell you,' she said, laughing a little
still and with her head on one side, her hair all hanging
down. 'I've changed my plans. Just this minute. I don't
know why I didn't think of it before.'

'What do you mean?'

'I just thought, why go back home when I finish in
France? I could come back to London, have a holiday.'

'But, darling, that would be wonderful,' Mrs Stankovich
agreed.

'I've been so worried. You can't imagine how worried
I was. But there wasn't any need. There's no reason on
earth why I can't come back to London.'

'I thought perhaps you'd other commitments, which
is why I didn't like to bother you.'

'No, I've no dates fixed yet. Next I'm scheduled for

is a summer festival: Newport, we have one every year. In July. But that's weeks and weeks away. You know, it seems so funny I didn't think of it before. I could laugh and laugh.'

'You've been mixing your drinks,' Mrs Stankovich accused. But gently. She wasn't really cross, so it didn't matter one little bit.

'Leaving the hotel this morning, one of those newspapermen said he'd heard something about my staying on - a rumour I guess, or he was bluffing. But it didn't strike me till just this minute why I shouldn't. Is that bad grammar?' she asked suddenly.

'I'm not sure.' And she said it over once or twice, and it sounded less grammatical each time.

'I wish you wouldn't. You remind me of a teacher I once had. I was desperately in love with her, and she never even looked my way.'

'Good heavens, you and your love affairs. Really in love?'

'Well. No. Just a crush I guess. But I remember I was pretty cut up over it. I suppose it was my first love affair.' 'All I ever hear about when you're in wine is your love affairs.' And, glancing quickly round first, tapped her nose with her finger. 'What I want to know is what are we going to do this afternoon?'

'Everything and nothing. Show me some London,' she added, thinking suddenly how nice that would be. 'Not the Tower or the British Museum or anything like that: some real London.'

'All right. Let's do that.'

So they paid the waiter, going halfs over it because one wouldn't let the other, and went out into the sunshine.

It was bright, and hot. But nebulous somehow, withdrawn, like she saw it through tears. She felt stupid, pretty nearly drunk. But it didn't matter: she liked the sensation. She liked the way the light looked, the way the air seemed to cushion her every movement. Like lying on a big, soft cloud. They went round all the little back streets and looked at theatrical masks and faces, at old prints and antiques, and embraced quickly in a narrow, shaded alley. A sudden, spontaneous coming together like they hadn't seen each other for ages. No one saw. (She had to keep reassuring Mrs Stankovich about this.) She wouldn't have cared if they had, didn't think so anyway. But it didn't matter much. They wandered out into the Charing Cross Road and listened to a busker doing a one man band, and played a bit in a pin-table room - though Mrs Stankovich hadn't wanted to go in: she'd never been in one before she said - but didn't win anything. And then, looking at a selection of paperback titles, she caught hold of Mrs Stankovich's hand suddenly and whispered where could she go to the toilet and Mrs Stankovich said there'd be one at the tube station, just a little farther down. So she said to wait for her right there, not to move an inch or she'd think she'd lost her. She wouldn't be a minute. But then, in the lavatory, was suddenly afraid something would happen to separate them, something dreadful. Like a fire, or a tidal wave. Yes, a tidal wave rushing down the Charing Cross Road. And was as quick as she could be and then ran all the way back. Yes. She was still there. Looking at the books. She was getting just a little bored, she joked, reading the same titles over and over. There was one, English Love Poems: they went in and looked at a copy, and Mrs Stankovich got it for her because there was one in there she specially liked. Andrew Marvell. Then they walked north again, and she bought Mrs Stankovich a little hairy spider with google eyes and pipe-cleaner legs at a souvenir shop. And Mrs Stankovich - because she said she thought he was cute - bought her a small doll dressed as a London policeman. It wasn't worth half the price but she liked it, and the book too, better than anything she'd ever been given before. She'd keep them always she said, leaving the shop, always. And then was afraid, didn't know why she'd said it like that. Sort of emphatic, like they were two people at an airport saying good-bye and not knowing when they would see each other again. But laughed it off because it was stupid getting scared like that when she was so happy. Nothing in the world could stop her coming back to London after France. Nothing. Not Cassidi, or anybody. Not even - oh, what? Not anything, that's all. She needed the rest, was due for one.

Then they crossed and had a cup of tea in one of those self-service places, and the tea was awful, and the shelf a clutter of unwashed cups and saucers. But she loved every minute of it, she told Mrs Stankovich, loved every sip of the lousy brew. Not that there was anything specially English about it: it could have been any old place, anywhere. But, she said, because she'd never been so happy. Only it had got late and they hadn't noticed: she was going to the school, Mrs Stankovich reminded her.

'Yeah. And then? What then?'

Well, Anthony was going to have supper with these friends of his. He was going straight there from the art school, after the evening class.

That'd be super. They'd have the whole evening together, and to hell with everything else.

No, she'd suddenly thought: could she meet her at the Burlington Arcade? She'd one or two things to get: some special cigarettes for Anthony. And she must go to Fortnum's. Did she know the Arcade?

Yes, she did. (But funny: till that moment, till Mrs Stankovich mentioned the Arcade, she hadn't even thought to ask where they'd meet. Somewhere, somehow, she just expected to find her. Like London belonged to them, had got suddenly small to accommodate just the two of them.)

To come at about six, Mrs Stankovich said. She'd wait at the gate, and then they wouldn't miss each other.

She went with Mrs Stankovich to the tube station, waited while she bought her ticket, then waved good bye. Mrs Stankovich, waving too, stepped on to the escalator and then was gone. She waited a moment, though she didn't know what for, then left the station, retraced her steps. The street seemed grey and cold and shut in, not at all the same. The sun had gone behind the buildings and the street was now a cool crevasse cut into the varied surface of the city. She felt suddenly exhausted. Her limbs were like lead, her eyes sore, and she was thirsty as thirsty in spite of the tea. But this was it: this was the school.

ANTHONY - SARAH

Ah, there she was. Crossing the street. (He'd come down specially: was beginning to wonder where she'd got to.) Glancing to the left, she swung gangle-legged, slim-hipped across the street. An easy, graceful action: her hair blowing back a little, away from her face. She'd slender, sculptural limbs: the bones very beautifully made. But reminded him too - crossing the street and her hair blowing- of a gangling, renegade young Jesus. A young Jesus in jeans, with largish, beautiful bony hands and feet. And eyes like an Indian God-figure. Only he didn't see them now. She'd a pair of dark glasses on and they drew blank somehow, cut him off from her, made him vaguely uneasy. There was no communication - that was it. He'd be talking to a pair of coloured glasses, not to her. Also, they accentuated this mystery quality she had. (One sensed a presence: rather like going into a church and looking along the nave and seeing, at the far end, those material symbols - but this was ridiculous.) There was this reluctance to disclose her identity, this inward-looking something or other. She was entire, yes. Quite complete, inviolate. The glasses made him aware too of her mouth: it seemed to have a significance, an identity all its own. And the partly healed wound there at the side of her nose.

She didn't see him until she was right on top of him, about to enter the building.

'Oh.'

And she stood a moment, apparently disappointed. Or she hadn't expected to see him perhaps? She stood quite still: only her hair moved. In the large, inscrutable lens of the glasses he saw a cut of pale sky, a diminished version of himself. They irritated him a little, the glasses. He rather wished she'd take them off.

'Hello,' he said. 'Please come in.'

And into the high, cool simplicity of the large entrance hall. No architectural embellishments: only, there on her left, a group of small plaster figures on a stand. The work, he said, of a rather promising last-year student.

'Shall we take the lift? Or would you rather walk?

'It doesn't matter really. I'd rather walk. Do you have a canteen or something?' she asked as they started up the stairs. 'I'm terribly thirsty.'

'Yes of course. But it'll be rather crowded.'

She smiled a little, but not looking at him:

'I'll risk it. I must get a cup of tea or something. Do you mind?'

'Not at all. We've plenty of time. It's all very humble of course.'

'Humble? Oh don't bother, I'm humble too.'

He didn't quite know what she meant by that - something distant in the way she addressed him, that curtly ironic tone he already knew. Very polite, but vaguely contemptuous. But something behind it all, something he couldn't fathom. It left him rather at a loss.

'The canteen is on the second floor, next flight up.' (She looked, in any case, rather like a student. He didn't think anyone would recognise her, cause her any embarrassment.) 'I've two tickets, by the way, for your concert tomorrow night. My wife and I are looking forward to going.'

'Oh I'm glad.'

What age was he?, she wondered. (They'd got to the landing and he held open a door that lead off into a passage.) She couldn't be sure. Fiftyish? Narrow, very clever face. Sensitive, intelligent, reserved - the type she went for in a big way when she was sixteen or so. Those qualities, along with the male presence, she at once responded to. But it was like, somewhere inside her, a little red light was going on and off.

He followed her into the canteen. The lights were on, though the sun came in on the far side. The large room was crowded and noisy and there was a continuous clatter of cups and saucers. He found them a vacant table near the top of the room, then went across for two teas. Standing in the queue, he glanced over at her. She'd put her bag on the table and was looking at a book. When he got back with the teas she smiled politely, thanked him.

'What are you reading?'

'Not reading really, just looking. Poems. A mixed bag.'
'Do you like poetry?'

She seemed to think this question irrelevant.

'Yes. Well, some. I don't know a lot. I'm not terribly literate really.'

She was playing with one of those ghastly dolls one got at the souvenir shops. Turning it round and round in a thoughtful sort of way, her elbows on the table.

'Do you like him?' she asked. Then smiled. 'You don't. I guess, like most Americans, I'm a sucker for souvenirs. I've a whole collection of them. Something from every place I've been.'

He laughed, but could think of nothing to say. He rather suspected that her mind was a lot quicker than his, and it threw him off balance somehow. That she was not intellectual, he already knew. Intelligent, yes: but not in the least intellectual. But it remained that in conversation the intellectual was often at a disadvantage: he'd never been good at small talk.

'What else do you like?' he asked, fingering the thick canteen cup.

She didn't answer at once, but thought about it. Still turning the doll, examining it carefully.

'I guess most of all I like music,' she said, fixing the glasses on him suddenly. 'More or less. It depends. Music though is a sort of universal language: I like that. It makes you feel good somehow.'

'Any particular kind of music? Well, folk music obviously,' he added quickly, feeling rather foolish. She did nothing to help: merely glanced at him.

'No particular kind. All kinds. I don't think people are honest when they say they like only one kind, one extreme or the other. Or, if they are, they're just snobs. Do you know what I mean?'

'Yes, I think so.' But he didn't agree with her at all, saw no sense in it.

'I think it's wrong to put a taboo on a type of music, to label it this or that, to say this is for you and this is for you. Provided it has some aesthetic value.'

He made a small movement with his head but she didn't know what it was supposed to mean. Maybe she expressed herself badly or something, because he looked like he didn't really understand. She sensed, too, certain reservations that he preferred to keep to himself. It was a cowardly kind of behaviour she didn't like: she wished people would say right out, no I don't agree. He was too polite of course, that was what made it difficult.

'I mean, if we were content just to say I don't like that guy's kind of music and left it at that - you know? Instead, we have to actively hate it. Like a bunch of kids. And that goes for all kinds of other things too, not only music'.

'Our intolerance, of course, is the cause of a lot of misunderstanding.'

He'd got through to her at last he realised, touched on something. She looked hard at him and for the first time it was as though the glasses had eyes behind them. And then she looked away, looked at the doll again.

'Yeah, that's true. That's what it's all about.'

'What about England?' he asked. Because somehow he felt he wasn't being fair to her, wasn't as interested as she'd believed him to be. 'Do you like England?'

'Yes, a lot. My father was born here of course, though his parents were Indian.'

'Yes, Jane told me. I thought there was something.'

'Spiritually I'm not an American at all. Americans are so bloody stupid. I just don't understand how we can be so vulgar. We don't seem to care how ignorant we are.'

But he questioned the wisdom of this because in many ways he saw her as very American. She'd all the confidence, the unconscious arrogance too, of the average American. She was so wrong headed in some things, that was the difficulty, seemed quite unable to see through her inventions. And impetuous, a little too damning in her judgements. But with all the best will in the world - he agreed with Jane there. There was this real interest in people, this real concern. In fact, desperately sincere. And, like most strong-minded people, quick to take offence if one didn't see things in quite the same light. Her sincerity, though, made him very aware of the flaws in his own character. Made him feel devious even. This mask he wore, this façade he'd put up against the world. This horny, complicated disguise the intellectual instinctively grew against the ridicule of his fellows. But she too, yes: she also hid something.

'Why,' he asked on a sudden impulse, and knew immediately he shouldn't have done, 'are you afraid?'

The hard, crepuscular lenses fixed on him again, sent

the light back at him.

'Afraid?'

'Forgive me if I was clumsy,' he said, fumbling with the spoon in his saucer. 'What I meant was, you seem to be keeping something back. Some essential part of yourself. It gives this - well, rather negative impression.' He smiled. 'Difficult to explain really. I hope you don't think me rude?'

'So how would you have me be?'

He spread his hands apologetically, smiling still.

She said nothing for a long time. She stood the doll on the table and looked at it. He saw only her profile, could read nothing from it. When she spoke again the bitterness of her words shocked him a little.

'I don't know what it is about professors,' she said wryly. 'But I've learned a lot one way and another from professors. Professors and pimps.'

'I'm sorry, I didn't mean - '

She looked quickly at him.

'Oh don't bother. It's all right.'

They sat a moment in silence. Then:

'How many students do you have here?' she asked, looking around the room. 'It's a pretty large place.'

'Yes, we seem to take more every year. I don't know how we find room for them. But we're hoping to expand. The sculpture department badly needs more space. Sculpture is very popular suddenly. More than ever before. Do you like sculpture? - but I think I already asked you.'

'Very much. I did some at college. If I had time I'd do a lot more.'

'Time must be rather a problem for you?'

'Yeah, a big problem. The biggest I have. But crazy,

because the wise guys are always saying about how it doesn't exist and things like that.'

He laughed. There was a certain relaxation of tension. If it hadn't been for the mistake he'd made asking her was she afraid he'd have taken her up on that. As it was, he just laughed.

'Yes, there is that. Do you like Dali? - or any of the surrealists?'

'Not as a painter. I mean, not from a painterly point of view. But I think his ideas are great. I wish I had as much imagination. Just like dreams, his pictures. I sometimes have dreams like that. Do you dream?' she asked. 'Some people say they don't, but I never did believe it.'

'Yes, I think so.'

But like he wasn't sure if it was correct to admit to having dreams. If she hadn't said about people saying they didn't dream, he'd not have admitted it. She hated his correctness, his good manners.

'Mine are so real, I know I do. All kinds of landscapes: townscapes too. And always a bit frightening. Have you ever been afraid of a landscape?'

'I'm not sure.'

'Oh you must be. I dreamed once about these miles of sand dunes, and there were these pylon things right across them but nothing else in sight. Only sand and sky and these pylon things. A grey sky, featureless - would you call it that? I don't know. Anyway, I was a little boy in the dream - it happens that way sometimes - and there were some others with me. And then this woman came walking, and I had this knife I was playing about with, and we frightened her terribly and there was no one to help her, and then I killed her.'

He just looked at her. He maybe thought she was loco and didn't know what to say.

'Anyhow, it was just a dream. What was so funny was I hate that kind of violence, any kind of violence. It's such a bloody waste of time, and I'm such a bloody coward.'

'Yes. Well anyway,' he said, putting back his chair, 'we had better go up. There's a students' exhibition in the upstairs hall - you remember I told you about it - but we can see that after. I'll show you the sculpture department first, while it's empty.'

They took the lift the next couple of floors or so and stepped out into a narrow, bright passage at the top of the building. Some pieces of sculpture were in the passage: there wasn't enough room inside, he explained.

There was one oddly angled room on the right as they went in. This, he said, was where the beginners usually worked. Except sometimes he had to take an evening class there if the part-timers were using the other room. This, on the left, was the casting-room - much too small unfortunately. But there was a good light, as she could see.

The room was splashed all over with plaster and there was a deep tank in the far corner. The benches were crowded with half-finished work, and under the benches was a tangle of lead piping and broken-up armatures. And, on the floor, the occasional yellow gleam of scattered shims among the sawdust. There was a smell of plaster, and gas, and soft soap, and burning Brunswick Black. There was no one about. Only in the room on the right, a man mixing clay in the bins.

The other room was shut right off. He pushed the door, kept it open for her. It was awkward because she had to duck under his arm to get by: they were both rather embarrassed, why he didn't know. Perhaps because he was conscious of the hard, slim form of her legs: noticed especially her bare, bony feet. Brown, and the toenails whitish. The whole of her was wonderfully sculptural - this was what he was thinking. And about her hair: the extraordinary colour of her hair. One thought at first it was brown, but it wasn't. Not quite. It tended more to red. And about her skin: but only a painter could have shown the living colour of her skin.

This was a much bigger room, though the students were apparently pushed for space. There were metal stands all around the room, the figures shrouded in plastic covers to keep the clay moist. In the centre was a low platform on wheels, with a movable table, and tall electric fires with their heads directed at the platform. But the fires were off just now, the platform empty. A flowered wrap spread untidily across the boards. There were shelves on all the walls except for right opposite, which was all window. Most of the students, he explained, had an LCC grant.

What was LCC?, she asked.

London County Council. Not the part-timers of course: they came for an hour or two in the evening only, certain evenings in the week, and mainly for their own amusement. A lot of old ladies: it was their one social evening in most cases.

'Yeah. Sad.'

'Other classes we have are the beginners, one day a week usually, and the intermediate classes. Other than that, it's all ours.'

He was speaking a bit fast, like he was nervous. And then would pause, grope for words before going on. He seemed terribly concerned to say the right things, to be precise, but without boring her.

'You mean the advanced students?'

'Yes. Those who choose to specialise in sculpture for the NDD.' He liked, too, some of the softer sounds in her speech: the U for instance in Student. And her voice was low toned, which took off some of the stridency of the accent. 'This, of course, provided they pass in the intermediate examinations.'

'Which take in a little of everything?'

'That's right.'

There was a pause, another embarrassed silence. She looked around the room, saw the sky and flat sooty roofs beyond the window. Right up here, she could still see the sun. You could go a long way, could go to the sun, if you jumped from roof to roof like in hopscotch. But when she looked at him again it was like someone had struck her, the way he was staring at her.

'Do you have anybody particularly promising, anybody really good?' she asked.

It was like he woke up suddenly, came to life.

'Yes.' He glanced at the figures, went across. He'd this short white coat on, and bare arms, and looked a bit like a doctor. A sculptor was the last thing she'd have imagined. She remembered she hadn't thought his work all that good. A bit slick. He was a better teacher perhaps? - it sometimes worked that way. 'A life figure is a good test I always think - but you know something about it?'

'A little.'

'This is a rather good figure.' Shaking the plastic sheet, with its inside mist of condensation, from the clay. 'He's not worried you see about what's on the surface, but about what makes the surface behave in this particular way.'

She looked at it carefully. And then she looked at the hand that held away the plastic sheet and she saw the hair on the wrist and how it changed direction across the bone and faded into incipiency on the back of the hand. And it struck her how familiar this was. It was so familiar she could have shouted out, but not gladly. She was back suddenly - with Houston or Frankie, it didn't matter which. He was more like Houston maybe. Not to look at, but the same appeal. A strong sexuality, but tempered by refined sensibilities. And that clever cynicism: the way he smiled, like everything was just too stupid. But it wasn't him, no. It was the hand. The hand started something going somewhere inside her head. She remembered the pubescent hair on Frankie Rosengarten's forearms - all fluffy like on a peach - and felt physically sick, she was so afraid.

She looked again at the figure, but said nothing. He knew one of them ought to say something but couldn't think what. So then it happened, as though someone had struck a match somewhere in the dark and he saw her all illumined. He'd a sudden exaggerated understanding of her, her person particularly. (And yet she infuriated him with her inscrutability, her odd mannerisms.) She smelt of the sun, and the warmth the sun had encouraged. But a rather impersonal smell, like a boy. And this taint of alcohol on her breath. He didn't like the alcohol smell but it didn't seem to matter. He saw the jewelled link in her cuff - she'd taken up the spatula left lying on the stand, made a few deft turns with it - and he needed to do something physical with her. The jewellery she wore seemed almost a part of her, inseparable somehow.

It all had to do with this something he'd felt when she'd crossed the street half an hour ago: all that was in his head still. But it frightened him that she could have this effect on him: something warned him against it. And yet he would, he must. Must take hold of her hand, like this. And it was as though some force attached his flesh to hers and burned it all away. She still held the spatula: he could feel the point of it in his palm.

'Would you let go, please?'

She spoke quietly but there was an edge to her tone which made him think again. Foolishly (because he saw it now as inevitable), he hadn't expected she would refuse. And hated himself for his stupidity, for not having anticipated her reaction. But was glad too, yes. Glad she'd refused. He let go her hand: neither spoke for a minute.

'I don't think you understand,' she said at last. And was fumbling in her mind for some further explanation, that she was already promised or something, because she was afraid he'd resent the cryptic quality of her words, would think she was after baffling or intriguing him, when he said:

'I'm terribly sorry. It was foolish of me.'

'Don't bother. It's all right.' She set the spatula firmly into the clay at the base of the figure. 'In any case I have to go now. I have an appointment.'

'I'll see you down.'

'No, it's all right. Good-bye.'

Shaking a little, she left the building. It was like everything was broken all in little pieces again and she couldn't get them to fit together. And she'd have to tell Mrs Stankovich: she'd feel dirty unless she told her.

Safe in another of those anonymous vehicles one hired

for a few shillings - was that right, shillings? - she thought about how she would tell Mrs Stankovich. She'd say it before anything else, and just like it happened. Not all neatly parcelled up. She'd say not to be angry but she had something to tell her. She'd be surprised maybe. So then she would say yes, your husband just made a pass at me but I didn't let him do anything. And what would Mrs Stankovich say to that? My poor darling, don't look so downcast. (Along those lines.) If I worried myself over Anthony's every little deviation from the straight and narrow I'd be a very silly woman. That it happened to be you was unfortunate, but not your fault at all. Something like that, she thought. She was so good, so kind. And she'd say, you're not angry with me then? (Frankie would have beat her blue.) And Mrs Stankovich would smile in that sad, amused little way she had and say something about - about what? Oh, some old thing or other. Something nice. Ah hell, was it worth it? Was it worth bothering? Time she got back to the hotel she'd decided it was and decided it wasn't half a dozen times. Claiming her key at the desk, she finally decided it wasn't. (She didn't want to hide it, but they'd so little time together now and it would mess everything up.) What she'd do right now was ring Stephen to see if she could have the car. And then maybe they would eat out somewhere and the pieces would all fall together again.

Among the envelopes she'd collected at the desk was a pencilled message they'd taken for her - a call from her agent in New York. (So where was Cassidi when the call came through?) Most urgent. He'd been offered a series of TV dates for when she got back. Four half-hour programmes, and these would be networked all over the country. Would she ring him back as soon as she could, or get Cassidi to ring him?

No she bloody well wouldn't.

Cassidi, as it turned out, was having a ball with the Press. He'd given instructions not to be disturbed - no calls, nothing - had been closeted this last hour or more. So let him get on with it: she wasn't seeing the Press, or anyone.

SARAH

She didn't get the car - he needed it again. (But she could definitely have it tomorrow. He promised. He'd garage it for her some time during the afternoon. After lunch then, all right.)

It didn't make much difference: they decided they'd eat out anyway. Something light. They neither of them wanted a full meal.

The Arcade was emptying already when she got there, and all pale late afternoon light. London turned her back on the affairs of the day, faced the lights and the music. Like a painted figure going round on a pedestal, her artificial eyes black and staring and the lights going on and off right in her deadpan face. They'd be closing the gates in a few minutes, Mrs Stankovich said. So they went quickly in and looked at the jewellery and the silver and the ivory and the figurines and tobaccos and the dolls all dressed up as historical characters. There wasn't a soul around, it had got so late, and their steps sounded all along the Arcade. There was one window with all these dolls, and there was a doll dressed as Katherine of Aragon in a high collar and black velvet and very proud looking and sad. 'She reminds me of you,' she said to Mrs Stankovich. 'Something: I don't know what.' And then wished she hadn't because Mrs Stankovich seemed suddenly afraid, stared at her. And there was another window with antiques and things and this small eighteenth century clock all gilt and enamel and it was like the clock formed a trembling drop there behind the glass, all shut away with the dust and the velvet, and the drop swelled like it would fall. But the clock had stopped, said another time altogether, so it didn't really matter and the drop didn't fall. They looked in another window and there was a gilt-gesso glass, one of those convex ones that made them look all head and eyes and big blobby noses, and their two selves in the glass together and it didn't matter. It didn't matter all the way back on the other side of the Arcade. It didn't matter passing the Royal Academy. Over the way was Fortnum's and Mrs Stankovich told her about the clock, how when it struck the hour Mr Fortnum and Mr Mason came out and bowed to each other and then went back and the little doors closed again. And it was so beautiful, the way she described it, she could hardly believe it. And Mrs Stankovich laughed and was happy again when she said will it do it now, for us? No, of course not: it had gone six. Then they looked at the motor cars in the BMC showroom and Mrs Stankovich laughed at her again when she said how she got a kick out of handling fast cars and was going to get herself either a Shelby Mustang or a Lamborghini when she went back. But then, walking with their shoulders touching, dawdling, laughing at everything, they passed the United

Arab Airlines office and there were these glass doors with curly snakes, and a big model aeroplane, and over the doors a sign that said to Fly Comet 4C Jet in big letters. And it was like everything fractured again, fell apart, began to hurry and turn and gather speed, and she looked at her watch suddenly and saw how late it had got and how little time they had.

Later still, after they'd eaten, they looked at the lights in the Circus. It was all pretty small scale after those at home, but a lot more kookie. They excited her like she'd never seen electric lights before. They jumped and blinked and totted up their slogans and then went dark and began all over again. There was the Guinness Time clock, and all the little stars winking on and off, and Coca-Cola, and Gordon's Gin, and the *Daily Express*. When they'd done looking at them, she signalled a cab with Mrs Stankovich's umbrella. Inside, she pressed up against her. The light kept moving across one half her face, sweeping on down and across the floor, and she was so beautiful in that nebulous sort of way. Nebulous because it was a crushed ice beauty with the low sun coming through, an impersonal beauty. It was like a drowned face, a dream face or something like that: you didn't even need to speak to it, it was so peaceful. (Only, behind the face, a pendulum swung and she remembered something about Dali, time, like it was years ago.) And the pale eyelashes - there where the light touched on them, coming, going, coming - bright like moth's wings. And, back behind the lids, the smiling calm of her deep eyes. She'd grey eyes: cool as rock pools.

'You know, I can't think what I'd have done this visit if I hadn't chanced to see you again in that coffee bar.

Doesn't it seem ages ago?'

'No, I don't think so.'

'It does though. Listen, I know I said it before, but with you everything noisy and clamorous and violent just falls away and I'm in a wood somewhere, and small leaves with the sunlight coming through them - the way it does, you know? Or bluebells after the rain. Have you ever been in a bluebell wood after the rain? Just like you: the smell, the colour, everything. You're a pale blue person, do you know what I mean?' This sounded kind of phoney, and she knew it, and maybe Mrs Stankovich knew it too. It was all an act - it must be, or she wouldn't know it. And yet she meant it, or something like it. Even if she wasn't completely sincere she believed she was, wanted to be rather, and that was what was important. (But, Jesus, how did she do it? How did she see it so clear, like it was someone else all this was happening to?) She looked away, looked at the little card in front that said to sit well back in your seat for comfort and safety. 'With you, I'm like I was before. Years and years ago. Or maybe not so long, I don't know. But, do you know what I mean?, clean. Last visit I went everywhere, did everything - I think I was stoned out my mind all the time. I mean the "in" places, you know? The clubs, the discotheques - the places you go to be recognised. Not because I wanted, but because they wanted. You know what they charge for a drink in those places? Five shillings for a tiddly one, or more than that. But it was my first visit and I had to go along with them. Suddenly I was a celebrity - that's a lousy word. 'Course, if you make the big time, you don't always have to do what they want. Leastways, I don't see why you should.' She smiled suddenly. 'You will come tomorrow night?'

'But, sweetie, of course. Why?'

'I don't know. I keep thinking you'll go up in a puff of smoke, like I dreamed you.' She reached up her arms suddenly, heard the rush of her clothing as she wrapped them around Mrs Stankovich's neck. She shut her eyes tight and moved her open lips across her face, and down to the corner of her mouth. And then, opening her eyes: 'I'll remember doing that always, the way it felt.'

Gently but hastily, Mrs Stankovich disengaged herself. Maybe she was afraid someone would see, the driver maybe.

'But, darling, a few days and you'll be back.'

They looked at each other a moment in silence. She thought again of the doll she saw in the Arcade.

'I meant all the while I'm in France,' she said. 'It's going to seem ages. I'll hate every minute.'

'All things pass. You wait and see.' She hesitated, still looking at her. 'Love too, darling. Love passes.'

'But you won't stop loving me while I'm there?'

'My sweet silly' (pulling herself together), 'if I didn't love you so very much I'd spank you for that.'

'Go on then.'

'You know' (smiling but serious), 'you're a real little masochist.'

'No, not with you. It's not the same as with a man.'

Mrs Stankovich looked hard at her, strangely, then looked out of the window. She had a way of looking sometimes like she wasn't sure if you were telling the truth but would give you the benefit of the doubt. It made her uncomfortable, made her feel dishonest: she couldn't think what to say. She cracked her knuckles a few times, examined her fingernails.

'You know what I'll be singing tomorrow night, what particular song?'

'No?'

'The one about Queen Jane.'

'Queen Jane?'

'Queen Jane Approximately. Listen.' She sang the words of the song into her ear, quietly. Then: 'Do you recognise it?' she asked. 'You should, because I sang it once before and you were there.'

'Yes. Yes, of course. The other night, at John's place.'

'You looked round the open door. But quickly, like you weren't sure.'

Mrs Stankovich laughed a little. 'Did I?'

'But that's your name, isn't it?, Jane. Funny. That I happened to be singing about you and you came.' Funny, too, that it never occurred to her to use her Christian name. It'd seem so wrong somehow: like calling your mother by her Christian name. It just wouldn't happen, she couldn't do it. Was that all right, she wondered? Or didn't she ought to feel that way? It maybe looked kind of funny, like she didn't care enough to use her Christian name. She was going to say something about it, but was too late.

'Coincidence?' Mrs Stankovich suggested.

'I'm superstitious. No, honestly. Don't you believe me?'

'I wouldn't have thought so.'

'Oh, but yes. This ring I wear, the gold one: I wouldn't leave it off for anything. I had it years ago, on my sixteenth birthday.' She thought a minute. 'Not all that long I guess: six years. But I don't seem to have accomplished much in that time.'

'But good heavens, you're rich and famous.'

'Anything of any real importance I mean. I sometimes wish I could do something big with my life, something that'd be good for everyone. Some kind of sacrifice, do you know what I mean? I hope that doesn't sound sloppy or anything.'

'But, darling, you couldn't possibly please everyone, no matter what you did. There'd still be those who wouldn't give twopence.'

'I don't know. It seems to me sometimes I could do something more.'

'Then you're a silly girl. Your songs give pleasure to thousands - what more can you give than that?'

She shrugged, smiled. (But strange that you could send a million people mad with just a smile. That was what was so bad about it: it gave you a feeling of terrible power. And one got so fed up getting what one wanted every time.)

'It doesn't seem enough, that's all. But I'm making myself afraid, talking like that. Tempting fate. What I value most right now is you and I wouldn't sacrifice you, not for anyone. I need you too bad.'

'What about tomorrow?' Mrs Stankovich asked. 'What's your programme, what do you have to do?'

'Nothing special. I've a run-through a short while before the actual performance, but that only lasts about an hour. They have to fix the balance and lighting plots and so on. They'll all be there: Cassidi, and the rest. Otherwise I'm more or less free. Leastways, normally I might rest or play a little -'

'Then you must rest. You mustn't think of doing anything different. As it is, you ought to be in bed. Does Mister Cassidi know you're running around town?'

'Oh him, he was in conference with the Press. I just

slipped out again, soon as I was ready. He'd probably forgotten all about me. He gets one hell of a kick out of that kind of thing, loves the limelight. He can have it.'

'Isn't he going to be cross when he finds that you're missing again?'

'So hell. He's not my keeper.'

'No. But the point is, you need some sleep.'

'All he's here for is to look after my hotel accommodation, to negotiate with the Press and that kind of thing, and to see I'm not bothered unnecessarily. He might have fixed up some TV dates if I was going to be here longer - I haven't said to him yet that I'll come back to London after France.'

'Hadn't you better do so?'

'I will, when I'm ready.'

They'd gone a long way in silence before she spoke again. She lay against Mrs Stankovich, with her head on her shoulder.

'Did I tell you I once had a dog and I called him Blue - there's a song goes like that. Blue?, they said. Yeah, Blue. But he's yellow, they said. It struck me then the way most people go about with their eyes shut. Most people, they can't see beyond their own noses. Like people who think about some things being normal and some things not - I just don't understand people who think like that. What's normal anyway? What does it mean? And what's abnormal about abnormal? Just because you ain't got your eyes shut like them.' She looked at Mrs Stankovich suddenly. It seemed the day had been terribly long, and she was so tired. She wouldn't be talking like this, about being superstitious and doing something big and what people thought and didn't think, if she wasn't so tired.

Tomorrow everything would be good again. Tomorrow she'd think to herself it wouldn't be so long after all before she got back to London. And how she had it to live for every minute she was away, the getting back. 'Someone, some journalist guy, once wrote about what he called my nobility. So maybe you wouldn't think, just looking at me, some of the awful things I done. I sometimes wonder was I brought up with wild dogs, or what.'

'Look' (reaching out and smoothing her hair back from her face), 'no more confessions. Are you very sleepy? I think you're half asleep.'

'All I wanted to say was I feel I just don't deserve to have found you, that I haven't done anything to deserve being this happy.'

'Every word of which is absolute nonsense. Are you going to come in?'

They were near to her place now. She wondered if he'd be there yet, whether she should go in or not.

'Will he be back yet, your husband?'

'I don't know.' Then, peering through the window as they pulled into the kerb: 'I don't think so, there aren't any lights.'

'Then I'll come in.'

'But only for a minute or two. You'll want some sleep if you're going to be any good tomorrow. We'll keep the cab, then he can take you back.'

ANTHONY

He was in the upper hall during the few minutes break in the evening class, stopped to look at some of the work.

The hall was almost empty: the lights were on. There was some good illustrative and commercial work, some good paintings too. One in particular caught his eye, a rather mysterious thing. Two young women, fully dressed, floating Chagall-like in a night sky. It disturbed him rather, that dream-like embrace. A quality of innocence, of dream-like innocence that excluded him somehow, left him out.

He heard someone, looked quickly round. Swan. He came through the double doors at the far end, sprang up the steps to the common room. A bit of a cad. A large, loose-bellied fellow with paint-smeared pants and incredibly soft spoken for his size. Had all the girls after him. Seeing him go, he thought again of Miss Kumar. Except for these few moments in the hall, he hadn't once forgotten her. Remembered, rather, his own ridiculous behaviour. Allowing for some exaggerated sense of his own attractions, some misconceived vanity, he could find no explanation for it. No (looking again at the two floating girls, one of whom vaguely resembled Miss Kumar), it was impossible. Impossible that he'd found her in the least - and yet not: she was sufficiently interesting, sufficiently attractive even. But wrong, wrong. Not at all the sort of girl - and that was it of course: much too young. Gawky, breastless, defensive: a woman's woman. Yes, absolutely. And it was this, he thought, which accounted for his sense of her untouchability. That oneness, that wholeness which had goaded him into action against her. Yes. Aware of her dissociation, baffled, he'd put her to the test. He'd been uncomfortable with her right from the start: she had to be vanquished. (But was he absolutely right in this? In his assumption of her wholeness? One jumped to conclusions so easily when one was looking for an excuse. He'd sensed her fear too, had been aware more than once of a façade similar to his own.) It disgusted him that he must come to this conclusion at last, that he had to come to a conclusion at all, but there it was. That same pride which - oh, a year or two ago now - had incited him against one of those dreadful young men Jane seemed to collect, to frighten the life out of him during a subsequent interview - of which Jane knew nothing.

'Hello, Stankovich.'

Swan. He'd come back, crossed the hall without his noticing.

'Oh, hello there, Swan.'

'I can't sell you a ticket I suppose?'

'What's that?'

'Folksong, at the Royal Festival Hall. Tomorrow night.'

'No. No, you can't. As a matter of fact I got two off one of your students a couple of days ago. Why? Can't you go?'

'Nope, something's come up. Never mind.'

'I'd try one of the students. Someone must want to go.'

'Yup. I'll do that. Do you like that painting? He's got some interesting ideas, that chap.'

'Yes, it's rather good.'

'Unusual sort of subject but treated in a rather interesting way, don't you think?' He laughed a little in that soft way he had, scratched the back of his neck. 'Never out of date of course: goes on all the time.'

'Yes, I suppose so.' And smiled too, but thinly, looked at his watch. 'I must get back to my class.'

'Yup. See you.'

But - good God, no. It couldn't be. But always together. Dinner together, this together, that together. Together in the firelight. And certain things Jane had said, certain things he'd seen. And yet it had never entered his head to suspect them, not when he'd surprised them together even. But a girl? Was it possible?

JANE

She was almost ready for bed when Anthony came in. 'Is that you, darling?'

He couldn't have heard. He didn't answer.

'Have a good time?' she asked when he came up at last. And then looked round. Something strange about him. She thought at first he'd drunk too much, but no.

'I found this downstairs,' he said. 'In the hall.'

He held something that shone suddenly, swung from his hand. A thin silver chain with a medallion. Of course: Sarah's. The miraculous medal she wore around her neck. And remembered the violence of her embrace when they said goodnight.

There were any number of things she could have said, any number of excuses she could have made. But she said nothing. Simply felt quite stupid.

'Oh,' she said at last.

'Whose is it? Yours?'

Of course he knew it wasn't. She looked away suddenly, tilted the glass a little so she could see better. (But was that the woman who was feeling all these things? It didn't seem real. That she could look so the same and yet be feeling all these things.)

'No. It belongs to Miss Kumar.'

He came up behind her, stood a moment. Then threw

the medallion down on the dressing-table. It struck the polished surface, writhed across it a short way. The link was broken. She took it up instantly, as though afraid it would come to further harm.

'When was she here?'

'Tonight.' And, turning suddenly: 'Darling, we're not going to quarrel about it?'

'About what?'

'Oh for goodness' sake don't be so tiresome. Must you behave like a schoolboy?'

'My dear, when have I ever behaved like a schoolboy?'

'Now. This minute.'

'No. I want an explanation, that's all.'

'An explanation?'

'Naturally. I want to know what reason we have to quarrel.' And, stopping her before she could open her mouth: 'Your words, not mine.'

Mechanically, she straightened the items on the dressing-table, put this tidy and that.

'I believe you know. Or there wouldn't be all this.'

He leaned on the back of her chair, his shoulders hunched. In the glass, she saw his beautifully sensitive hands: one either side of her, the knuckles white.

'All right. What's it all about? What's been going on?'

She questioned his reflection.

'Going on? Have you no imagination?'

'Then she's your lover?'

It was vulgar, it was cheap, it was dirty. The way he used the word. Oh yes, she knew what he suffered. How he was angry because he sensed this was as near perfect as a relationship could be. That he couldn't comprehend it, felt excluded. It wasn't the same as if she'd taken a man.

A man's relationship with a woman was almost always destructive. A man must demoralise, degrade, must strip a woman of her dignity for very fear of her. Sex, from a physical point of view, didn't come into it the way it did with a man. Which, perhaps, was why Anthony couldn't tolerate these relationships: it was all a bit above his head. Between herself and Sarah there was nothing of the strain she associated with heterosexual relationships. It struck her now for the first time what a different thing it was, her love for Sarah. And he wasn't going to turn it into something vulgar, something cheap, merely to avenge himself. She knew quite positively at this moment she no longer felt anything for him. It was gone, whatever there had been in the past - had been gone a long time. And just three minutes ago she'd been so happy, hadn't dreamed or anything like this, anything so cheap as a showdown.

'Lovers? Yes, I suppose so. But I wonder, Anthony, if you know what it means - to love?'

'Don't give me all that poppycock. I want to know what happened.'

She turned in surprise, faced him at last.

'You want to know what?'

'I want to know what happened.' He tightened his grip on the chair, lost patience suddenly. 'Damn it, I want to know.'

'I don't understand.'

He flung away, lit a cigarette and walked about the room. Up and down, up and down.

'You don't expect me to believe that? Sex, that's what I'm talking about. I want to know what happened between you sexually.' He stared at her suddenly, with that incredulous little smile of his. 'What could you possibly want with a woman? What could make you want a woman sexually?'

She turned her back on him again. It came to her, now, that she'd never thought to analyse it - hadn't looked at it that way at all. It had all been as natural as breathing.

'No Anthony. I'm not going to let you speak about it in that way. Falling in love with Sarah was quite as natural as falling in love with a man. I didn't even think to question it. It simply happened. But not the same as being in love with a man - you've got it all wrong, know nothing about it. Different. In what way, I don't know. Perhaps in that passion is controlled by a deeper, a more basic sentiment. Sex doesn't come into it really. I love her as I might have loved a daughter - more than that I can't say. Only that I feel it will last.'

'But why should it happen at all? How did it come about?'

'How do I know? These things just happen. I wish you wouldn't smoke in here, darling,' she added. And knew at once that it was ludicrous right in the middle of all this, that he would jump on it and use it against her.

'Yes, that's about as sensible as anything you've said tonight. That just about sums the whole thing up. What's smoking in the bloody bedroom got to do with it? My God, Jane, d'you think I'm not serious? Do you think I'm enjoying myself?' He'd stopped his prowling, stood a little way off. 'I forbid you to see her again.'

She got up, walked away from him.

'Don't let us behave like children for goodness' sake.'

'Children! Hell!' He snatched up the chain suddenly, tore it apart. The medallion flew off: she heard it rattle away under the wardrobe. 'I'll show you what a child I can be. That bloody little -'

He broke off. No longer angry, but like an embarrassed little boy: fidgeting, twitching. At the back of him, in the glass, she saw his limp fair hair and the hollow at the base of his skull, and it was as though there were two of him: the one in the glass, and the one facing her. But what on earth was the matter with him? What had taken the wind so suddenly out of his sails? Something she'd said?

'What is it? What's the matter?'

He hesitated, undecided. Then threw his cards on the table.

'There's something I ought to tell you, Jane.'

'What, now?' (Some woman he'd messed about with: she ought to have known, she'd heard it all before.) 'Tonight? I don't see what it has to do -'

'A lot. I don't know how to put it really, but this afternoon, when she came to the school -'

No, she didn't believe it. She'd ring her: now, this minute. Make him speak to her. But then she remembered little things. Little things Sarah had said at the beginning that had given her the impression she was something of a good-time girl. But no. She knew what that was all about: the girl had been afraid, hadn't entirely trusted her. She had forgiven all that long ago. But there'd been something tonight, yes. Something in her behaviour. In the cab, she remembered. At one point - something she'd said about remembering always what it was like when she kissed her - she'd half suspected her. And all that nonsense about not deserving to be happy: that one wouldn't think, just to look at her, some of the awful things she'd done. She would insist on that, had spoken of it before. And it was a fact that she wasn't as sure of Sarah as she was of herself. Never had been. She was so young, so unsettled. There

was, if she was absolutely honest, a certain amount of
strain attached to their relationship. She worried about
the girl terribly - both in connection with herself, and for
her own sake. But it was simply too ridiculous, this story
of his. She couldn't even entertain the idea.

'You're wasting your time. I know it to be untrue.'

'I'm afraid you misunderstand me. It was my fault.'

'What?'

'It came over me, the way these things do. I can't
imagine why. I didn't want it any more than she did.'

But it appalled her, this confession.

'And Sarah?'

He shook his head.

'No. Nothing.'

He hadn't of course known the position at the time
- whatever he might have suspected. In which case she
could hardly make an issue of it. (He'd have liked that
perhaps?) But that he'd dared! Her mouth was suddenly
dry, bitter.

'But why?'

'I don't know. I can't think. She was close to me and -
and I was curious, that's all.'

Yes, he was telling the truth. But that he'd dared!
(Which was ridiculous, of course.) And why hadn't
Sarah told her? She hadn't thought it worth while she
supposed. It must happen to her all the time. No longer
angry, no. Her common sense took over. She couldn't
possibly blame him: it was just one of those things. Good
God, she was used enough to his infidelities. A complete
coincidence that of all people it had been Sarah.

He relit his cigarette, which had gone out.

'No, I can't think why. Any more than I can understand

you. Why you fell for a guitar-bashing female drunk I can't imagine.'

'Anthony!'

'Every time I've seen her she's been drunk. All that fine talk - and look at the way she lives.'

'Please, no. You don't know her at all.'

He looked up suddenly.

'And how well do you know her?'

'What do you mean?'

'What I say.'

'Better than you.'

'And how better is better? What do you really know about her? Nothing.'

'Anthony, please.'

'No. Not please. Don't say anything more. I've made up my mind: I forbid you to see her.'

'Look, you will have to get it into your head that you can forbid nothing. I'm not going to allow you to stand between us, with your threats and abuse. She needs me, and I can't possibly stop seeing her. Not for you, or anyone else.'

'Needs you? Ha! And what about me? I don't come into it I suppose?'

'You have your women, your affairs. I don't stand up like a judge and forbid you to see people.'

'Affairs, yes. That's exactly what they are. Nothing more. Those women mean nothing to me.'

'No? Have you never wondered what they meant to me when I first married you, what I felt when you came in smelling of another woman?'

He drew himself up a little, as though she'd slapped him in the face.

'Nevertheless they mean nothing to me. I love you, Jane.'

'No, Anthony. You're not going to burden me with that. Also, you're just a little too late. I've no conscience now, no scruples whatever.'

'You mean you'll persist in this?'

'Persist in it? I'm in love, Anthony, in love,' she cried, suddenly exasperated. And then: 'Yes. She's coming back to London after the French tour, and I mean to go on seeing her. I can't imagine why this should change anything. You have your little affairs, I have mine.'

'Is that what you call it? In that case I suppose I can hope for you to tire of her?'

'No, that wasn't what I meant. And you know it. I love her, so for goodness' sake let that be an end to it. I'm tired. I'd like to go to bed if you don't mind.'

'Yes, I do mind. I mind very much. I object to the whole thing. I'm not going to be cuckolded by a bloody woman.'

'If that's the way you feel then I must leave, that's all.'

'Leave? That's what you think.' He came and leaned towards her across the bed, his knuckles pressing down into the mattress. 'I tell you, Jane, if you left me it'd be for nothing. She'll no more come back to London than fly in the air.'

She turned her back on him.

'For God's sake leave me alone, Anthony. Leave me alone.'

SARAH

At intervals all next morning she tried to get Mrs Stankovich on the phone. She couldn't think why she didn't answer. Had she gone out, or what? But she must get back some time, and she hadn't said anything about not being there all morning. But no reply. Not the first time, or the second, or the third. And, soon as she got through, the phone cut out suddenly like someone took the receiver off.

She had to keep going into the bathroom to call Mrs Stankovich because Cassidi was with her: talking, talking, talking on the phone to New York. (Why didn't he go some place else? She was thinking only last night he was beginning to know his place with her: he hadn't said a damn word about where was she and that.) She didn't like to use the one in the bedroom in case he overheard something. In the bathroom, she could run the tap. After five or six tries she rang down for a bottle of Martell and when it came poured herself a shot and lay down on the bed and tried to think it out sensibly. But it didn't seem any satisfactory answer could be got: she couldn't think what had happened, and listening to Cassidi yakkety-yaking next door didn't help any. So then she got off the bed and went to the bathroom and tried the number again, but still no answer. Then the Press and Public Relations rang through and said that there was a young lady from one of the weekly music papers on the phone, and wanting an interview - would she see her? But she said no, she wasn't seeing anyone. Didn't matter who it was. And then called the switchboard and told them the same. Not to put any calls through. Oh, only if a Mrs Stankovich rang. If she rang, put her through. But no one else. She wasn't seeing anyone. She was resting and didn't want to be disturbed. And then she drank another glass of brandy. And then, like someone told her she must, spoke into her ear, she got up and went into the bathroom again. 'What's the matter, honey?' Cassidi joked when she passed. And then, into the phone: 'No, Sarah. Yeah, well, we could fix up the venues later. Main thing is -'

She didn't wait to hear any more: she wasn't bothered. (But what venues? If he was thinking of another tour, he'd better think again.) Someone lifted the receiver at the other end: the ringing stopped. Her heart began to beat so fast she could hardly breathe. She didn't dare believe someone would answer.

Someone did. But it was him, not her.

Yes?

She bit her lip, turned the cold tap on. It made a dry little coughing sound, then the water began to run. Next door she could hear Cassidi talking, talking. Her head ached. And she felt like she was choking, could hardly get the words out.

'Is Mrs Stankovich there, please?'

Who was it?

She hesitated. She'd a feeling if she said her name the game was up. She heard the water going down the waste.

'Sarah Kumar.'

He was sorry, Mrs Stankovich wasn't at home.

She was going to ask where was she then?, but he cut her off. Just like that. Right in the middle, like he wasn't bothered. What the hell? What was it all about? Had she done something wrong? Everything was all right last night. Then why didn't she want to speak to her? She was at home, she was sure. He was lying when he said she wasn't there. But why? Had she told him to say that, or what? The more she thought about it the less coherent it got. It was all a tumble. All she could do, back in her room, was keep filling her glass and walking about and thinking no, it'd be all right in a minute. And then suddenly her heart would go down to her boots and she knew something was wrong. Mrs Stankovich was at home, asleep still maybe, but as soon as the phone went out came his hand and took the receiver off. She had to lie on the bed a while again: things were going round a bit, and it was a sort of shock to her when she allowed at last that something must be wrong. The walls kept falling away and the ceiling kept going slowly round and round. Then she knew she couldn't bear it any longer but must do something, must go to her, must see for herself. He couldn't refuse her entry: he wouldn't go as far as that. So she said to Cassidi she was going down for something to read (he just nodded his head, looked right through her: he was too tied up with whoever was at the other end), grabbed her coat and hurried out. Sliiip. Round the door she went, like castor oil. She'd left the door open, heard him call after her but she shut her ears to it. She must get a taxi: that was all she knew. A taxi as quick as possible. And then the taxi would take her to Mrs Stankovich and everything would be all right again. But she couldn't get a cab: they were all hired. It was like everybody wanted a taxi suddenly and that there were fewer than usual, not enough to go round. The guy in the uniform kept on apologising, said to wait and he'd get her one down the street. But he was gone so long, and people were looking at her, and she was scared to death Cassidi would pop up any minute now, so she didn't wait. She began to walk. Where, she didn't know. But if she kept walking she'd maybe see a taxi and then it would be all right. But money. Jesus, she hadn't got any money for a cab. Not enough money. There were three coins in her pocket, and a nail file. That's all. A shilling and a sixpence and a threepenny piece. It'd cost much more than that to get to Hampstead. And she came without her bag: there wasn't much English money in it anyway. (And without the shades too, but she wasn't bothered about that.)

She walked and walked then came to Trafalgar Square. She didn't know how long she'd been walking. Only that everyone seemed to be going the opposite way and kept knocking her off the pavement. There were plenty of cabs - but no, she hadn't enough money she remembered. Did she have enough for the subway? But it was only a minute ago she'd looked to see how much money she had: why did it seem so long? There was the Column. Black, but not so tall today. Sarah climbed up on a mountain and was playing to thousands and shouting. Instinctively, she fingered her nose. It didn't hurt at all. Up to now it had still hurt but now it didn't hurt a bit, not even when she squeezed it. She couldn't feel it at all. Like when you got pins and needles in your arm and it was just dead. But did anybody ever get pins and needles in their nose? Mountains, fountains. Somebody had pushed her face into the wall. She had hold of him now, she'd break his neck. Which way? Up there, on the right. If she went up there, she'd maybe find the tube station. But she seemed to be in everybody's way, and a man laughed at her, and a woman stood still and stared at her like she was something that had crawled out the cheese and then said 'disgusting' and something about a policeman so she went on quick as she could, crossed the street. And there were trees and a statue of Henry Irving and then nothing for a while, nothing she remembered, just a blank, and then the tube station. (She said it, in her head, in an English sort of way: tube station. The way Mrs Stankovich said it.)

She fell down the stairs. It was when she did this she realised she was drunk and that was why the man had laughed and the old lady had said about disgusting and why she couldn't feel her nose or anything else. She fell head first, face down, and the few coins she'd had rolled away somewhere and she just lay there a minute not quite sure what had happened to her. The stairs were dark and dirty and there were phone booths at the bottom. Then someone, coming down after her, said are you all right? And someone else got her under the arms and stood her up. And she laughed and said, yeah, fine. Only she'd lost her money, she said: she didn't see it anywhere. If she didn't find it she wouldn't have enough for her tube fare. So they had a look round for her but couldn't see it either. You wouldn't believe, she said to the man who'd helped her up, but I got thousands in the bag (she meant to say bank, but it didn't happen that way) and nothing to pay my tube fare. How much did it cost to get to Hampstead? The man said he didn't know really, and went rather red, and scratched his nose, and seemed terribly embarrassed by her. Then he felt in his trousers pocket and said here was five shillings: she could get to Hampstead with that. It was all in different kinds of change and seemed a lot of money to her, and she said something about sending him a cheque and he was terribly embarrassed again and smiled a thin smile and hurried off. But all the people who'd stood around when she fell down still stood around, and stared at her. One of them said she was a Yank. Someone else said she was drunk. Someone else said Yanks were always drunk. She couldn't explain

she wasn't drunk: she couldn't be bothered. She must get
to Hampstead. Where did she go to get to Hampstead?
There was a ticket machine just around the corner from
the lockers, and ticket offices, and escalators going down
in all directions. She went and read the ticket machine
but it jumped up and down and she couldn't see what it
said. Only big red numbers. Fourpences and sixpences
and that. So she put a shilling of the money given her
into the one that said a shilling and a ticket jumped out
at her like it was angry for being bothered and she took
hold of it gingerly and looked around again. People were
knocking her all over the place and someone trod hard on
her foot but it was like her feet were dead too: she didn't
feel a thing. Another somebody knocked the ticket out
her hand while she stood looking, didn't even bother to
pick it up, and she had to grope around for it and later
had to be stood up again because the ground was so safe
she couldn't let go. Which stairway? There were several.
Maybe that one. (She didn't seem to have hurt herself
when she fell down the stairs either. She couldn't feel any
bruises or anything.) There was a box where you showed
your ticket at the top of the escalator, and a man with
a cap reached out for hers. And he was going to punch
it only he looked at her again, looked harder. Was there
something wrong?, she wondered. Maybe if you were
drunk they didn't let you on the subway here.

'Are you all right, Miss?'

She bit in her lip. 'Oh. Yeah.'

So then he punched her ticket, but he didn't give it
back to her. He held on to it and looked at her again.
A whole lot of hitch-hikers had piled up behind, and
other people too, and some pushed past, holding out their

tickets to show they had one. Others just stood and stared.

'Oh,' he said. And it was like an echo of what she'd said. 'You're Sarah Kumar, blow me if you ain't. I never forget a face. You was in the paper.' If she went down, he said (in that loud explaining way English people had when they spoke to foreigners), she'd see the posters. They'd put posters up down there. (Up?, down?, which?) Telling all about her concert. Well fancy that. Blow him down. She didn't want to blow him specially, though she didn't like the way he'd looked at her at first, but all the people behind began to talk and there was a woman saying 'you know, on the TV' like she couldn't believe her eyes. And she called out to her friend buying a ticket, quick, it's Sarah Kumar, and she was quick. A lot of people were quick: the hitch-hikers too - a party of French kids with rucksacks and badges all over their sleeves. They knew her at once - 'l'Americaine, oui: folksinger' - and were wildly excited.

She ran. She broke through the crowd, pushing people out of the way, and ran for the exit. (It must have been raining when she came because her hair was wet and her feet were muddied. The thin sandals weren't any protection.) Which was stupid because a lot more people looked and then recognised her, or else thought she was an escaped criminal, and ran too. And got her up against this Moss Brothers show case that had all golfing gear in the window and crowded round. Kids mostly. The bowler hat brigade, now they knew she wasn't a criminal, kept well back and tried to look like it was all a bit beneath them but anything for a laugh old boy, anything for a laugh. Most trouble she had was from the French hitch-hiker kids: if it hadn't been for them she'd have gotten away.

But they weren't in the least embarrassed, treated her like she was street litter. Why the hell didn't someone do something to get her out of here? She'd be crushed to death in a minute, or bald and naked or something. They were stripping her like a Christmas tree. She had to keep throwing up her arms to stop them from cutting hanks of her hair, and when she did that they cut pieces out of her coat. And then they grabbed at her pants and shirt. They didn't want autographs or anything: they wanted her, bit by bit. She'd never been so scared. Sarah, Sarah, they kept shouting. But like her name didn't mean anything to them, like they wanted her blood instead. And every time they shouted out she lost something else. Rrrip! Like in a Charlie Chaplin film, but shown the wrong way round: everything rushing backwards. She felt weak as a baby, couldn't do a thing for herself. All she could do was keep them away from her hair. ('Cut your hair and they won't wanna know ya,' Cassidi had said once. Joan Baez cut her hair, Julie Felix cut her hair, they wouldn't wanna know them either. The hair is you: they'll all be growing their hair.') And while she was doing that they cut all the buttons off her blouse with their little camping knives, and snatched off the links she wore in her cuffs, and her sandals, and even tugged at the zip fly in the front of her pants. She shouted out something about get off me, for Jesus' sake, but couldn't make herself heard above the gaggle. And they got hold of her hands and pulled her rings off and tried to get her bracelet off too, but it stuck at the knuckles, cut into her skin.

One of the bowler-hatted men must have called someone, must have seen it had gone further than a joke, because some porters came and after a struggle broke the crowd up a bit and she was able to tear herself away. Only safe place she could think of was the ladies lavatory: there was one just across. She didn't know how she got there, everything was rolling about so, but she did and when she did she locked herself in the one at the end and leaned against the door. She wanted to be sick and to go to the toilet and to cry and didn't know which to do first, she wanted to do them all so badly. So she was sick in the toilet and wetted the floor and cried all at the same time. Her head thumped like it was going to break right open, and her face burned, and her clothes were in shreds. She didn't know what to do, just leaned against the wall and cried. Cried for what seemed ages. And when she'd finished crying began to think what to do. There was a big, glazed window on one side. She couldn't see much through it: only a greyish light and what she thought must be part of a roof and wall. The wall went right up, farther than she could see. It'd be stupid anyhow, crawling out of a window. In here there was a strongly antiseptic smelling roll of paper, a slant of yellow electric light on the white tiles, and a grey painted door with all kinds of things written on it. Rat bag. Tisgay. Andrew Smith. What did Tisgay mean? She tried spelling it round another way but still it didn't make sense. So then she got the nail file out of her pocket - it was still there - and thought a minute, and then carefully scratched I hate Frankie R. because she couldn't bother with writing Rosengarten, it was too long. And still hadn't thought what to do.

Later, someone rapped violently on the door. (She didn't know how much later: her head still went round and round.) She nearly hit the ceiling, and her heart began to thump fast. It was the woman attendant, and she sounded like a prison wardress. She said what was she doing in there?, hadn't she finished yet? She'd had more than her penny's worth.

Yeah well, suppose -

'Difficult,' she said from the other side of the door. And laughed. And then thought it wasn't funny at all, it was revolting. What was the matter with her? What would her parents have said.

But was anyone there?, she wanted to know. Any people?

'People? What people? If you don't come on out of there, Miss, I'll call a policeman to you.'

'Policeman?' In a thick, foreign accent. 'What is policeman?' She unlocked the door all the same and came out because a policeman was someone she didn't want to meet right now. She didn't want to meet anyone. The woman looked her down and up like she was a thief or a murderer or something, and then looked into the toilet and swore some awful language and said about the smell and said she had a mind to get her to clean it up herself and if she didn't clear off - O.R.F, she pronounced it - she'd call a policeman for sure. She knew where she could find one, oh yes. There was always a policeman just outside. And look at her clothes then: what had she been doing to herself? All cut up like that and no buttons on her blouse and no shoes on her feet. She was one of those beatniks, eh? Well she'd show her what she thought about beatniks if she didn't take herself off.

She wasn't a beatnik, she said. She was Sarah Kumar.

'Sarah bloomin' who?' And laughed in her face. But it was nice to talk to someone who didn't give a damn who she was: she wasn't in the least offended. Instead, she held out her hand and said good-bye. The woman looked at her like she was loco. She'd a big square face, heavy jaw, and arms like a wrestler. The big face was like a haunch of bacon she thought, feeling sick again, and it swung before her like a pendulum. And yet she didn't hate the woman: she could have cried on her bosom. Which was big enough, God knows. Big enough for two.

'A joke,' she said. Leaning against the wall, she was so tired suddenly. 'I got my coat caught in the door of a train, and they took my buttons because I hadn't the money to pay for my ticket. That's a sad story, isn't it? You know about paying with shirt buttons, don't you? Well that. But here's two shillings for your trouble: it's about all I have.' She pushed off from the wall. 'Do you have any kids? No. Okay.'

And left the woman gaping after her.

Maybe there was a phone box here? Yeah: where she fell down the stairs. She could try phoning again and if she got him and he said Mrs Stankovich wasn't at home she'd want to know when would she be back please? Yes. There were a whole lot of phone boxes. And a coloured porter washing the floor outside with a disinfectant. She hated the smell, was glad when the door squeezed to. But the door was stuck or something: it didn't quite close. The porter was looking funny at her through the glass, and there was a draught down the steps, and the smell of the disinfectant sickened her. But here was the slot where one put the coins. She rang through and waited. It went once or twice then stopped, and she heard Mrs Stankovich. She spoke cautiously, like she was looking over her shoulder.

Yes? Who was it?

'Me.' She couldn't say anything else because her throat choked up and she wanted to cry. Then, because there was no answer: 'Sarah.'

Silence again.

Darling, she said at last. (But like she couldn't think what to say next.)

'What's wrong? Why weren't you there before? I kept ringing, and nothing. And then I got him and he said you weren't there.'

But that was nonsense! She'd been in all morning. At least, she came down late: she hadn't slept well. She'd heard him answer the phone - was just coming down as a matter of fact. He'd said it was nothing, someone at the school.

'But I was ringing all the time before that, I was ringing all morning. And the phone went each time, and then it was like I kept being cut off.'

No, she hadn't heard anything. She'd slept late. She couldn't understand it at all. No, no: it was all right. There was nothing. Yes, of course. (And tried to laugh.) Perfectly well.

'There is something. I know there is. What's the point of keeping it back?'

Oh they'd quarrelled last night, that was all. He'd found out about them, made a scene. But it made no difference whatever: she'd simply ignored it. But was she all right? Was something the matter?

'Look, I got to see you. I was coming, only when I got out I hadn't any money on me. It was like a bad dream. It was terrible. And then I was danced on by a mob here at the subway and I hid in the lavatory.'

But where was she now? Was she all right? 'At the

station still. I don't know what to do.'

But what on earth was she doing there? She'd come, she said. (Without waiting for an answer.) Which station? Where?

She said where, and that she was in a phone box by some steps, and to come quickly, please.

She was to wait there, exactly where she was, and she'd come at once.

'But what about him? Is he there?'

No, he'd gone. He went just as she came down. It made no difference anyway, she had to get a few things. She wasn't to worry. Just to stay where she was.

'Yes.' And bit her lip because she thought she was going to cry again. 'But hurry. You will hurry, won't you? Only I have that bloody concert tonight, and I have to be there for the run-through.'

Yes. She'd only be a few minutes. But why she had to get herself into a mess like this she couldn't think: it was too bad.

Slowly, she put the receiver down. The relief was too much. But then, so it wouldn't look funny, she began to go through the directory. Like she was looking for a number. It was the longest wait she'd ever waited but Mrs Stankovich was there in just under quarter of an hour. She seemed momentarily shocked out of her mind when she saw her, like she'd stepped into the nightmare too. What had she been doing to herself?, she wanted to know. What on earth had she got up to?

'I'll tell you all about it. Let's get away from here first.'

She wanted to throw herself into her arms, to hide herself in her, to cry like a child. But not here. She had to get away from here.

'Darling, you're shivering. Are you cold?'

'Yes. I don't know. There's an awful draught blowing down those stairs.'

Mrs Stankovich looked at her a minute, then she looked all round like she couldn't think where they could go. And holding on to her arm like she was afraid someone was going to take her from her. She looked strained and tired and somehow desperate.

'Darling, stand up. Stand up, do,' she kept saying as she looked around. 'I think we'd better get a taxi. But I can't think where to: I don't know where we can go.'

'I don't care about where we go. I just want to be with you,' she tried to explain.

'Yes. Yes, I know, darling. But we have to go somewhere. Do try and be sensible. Wait in the phone box again, just as you were. I'll call a taxi.'

Waiting, she was swept again by nausea and was cold and hot all at once. She didn't know what she was doing. It was like, now Mrs Stankovich was here, every ounce of resolution was gone. She was tired, and it felt like there were no bones in her body. Wherever she moved her hand - the coin box, the phone, the looking-glass - it left a damp print that slowly evaporated. She kept doing this, just to see it come and go again. But then a sudden awareness of herself in the glass, like it was someone she didn't know. Peering in at her, curious. Heavy-lidded, glassy black eyes that seemed to send the light right back at her, they were so bright. Just a surface. And stopped somehow, like there was a wall behind them. And straggling hair, plastered down with wet, and her mouth open like an idiot. And drooling saliva all over the place. She thought she was going to be sick again but only the saliva came, hung like a glittering needle, and she had to let it fall because she hadn't got a handkerchief either. It slipped over the shiny stuff of her coat, ran down somewhere. What had happened to Mrs Stankovich? Why wasn't she here to give her a handkerchief? She'd been gone ages. She hadn't anything, anybody. Oh to God she could lie down and go to sleep somewhere. So cold. Her feet so cold. She looked down at her bare feet and they were funny-looking things, like they didn't belong to her. Big and bony and funny-looking. She was funny-looking all together she thought, staring in the glass again.

But Mrs Stankovich didn't mind: Mrs Stankovich loved her. Yes (crying and choking, dashing the tears away with the back of her hand), Mrs Stankovich loved her in spite of everything.

Or because of everything maybe. Yes.

It made no difference, Mrs Stankovich had said, that he'd found them out. (Mrs Stankovich all tired and strained and desperate, and looking all around like she didn't see anything.) So when she got back from France it would be all right. Everything would be all right. And she wouldn't want to drink or anything. (This was what she must stop, this always being stoned. But how much had it got to do with being unhappy, overworked? - that was the thing.) Yes. It was all going to be all right. And the nausea was passing. And here was Mrs Stankovich again.

But, momentarily, she was afraid to come out the box.

'All those people: have they gone?'

'But darling, there's no one here.'

'There was before.'

'Before what?'

She stared at Mrs Stankovich a minute, then

remembered.

'No, I mean before I rang you. I was getting mixed up. There was a whole pack of them, howling for my blood.'

'Come along. Don't be silly.'

Mrs Stankovich walked her up the steps and out into the air. It was grey and raining. There was a news stand at the side: she suddenly remembered seeing it as she went down. An old man selling papers, and a placard with something daubed on it. And a cab chuckling at the kerb and the rain dribbling off it. A taxi to take them to heaven. God bless mother, God bless dad, and send them to heaven in a taxi-cab.

Mrs Stankovich had reached out and was putting the hair back from her face.

'Darling, listen to me a moment. We have to go somewhere. Where would you like to go?'

'Heaven.' And she laughed a little, looking into her eyes. But she had to explain better, she realised. Had to explain she was thinking of that old jingle, or Mrs Stankovich would think she was stupid. Only it was too much bother, so she just said: 'Anywhere with you is heaven.'

'I think I'll have to take you back to the hotel. Would that be alright? Would you like that?' Taking a handkerchief out her bag and blotting at the saliva on the front of her coat, on her face. 'In any case, it's getting rather late.'

'Yeah, that'll do. I'm not bothered specially.'

JANE

She said nothing at all, only looked stupid as she helped her off with her clothes. She'd run a hot bath for her, was going to get her into it in the hope of sobering her up a bit. (It had been so terrible when they got to the hotel. She'd had to explain to Cassidi, who'd been going out of his mind, to make excuses for her, to partly invent in order that he shouldn't be too cross with her, and to ask would it matter if she went up with her - she'd get her into a hot bath and then to bed. She'd never been so embarrassed, not for years. Had felt herself compromised somehow.) The small room was full of steam: they stood in a rising vapour. There was a big tablet of scented soap in the soap holder, and a smell of warm towels and toothpaste. That extra clean, impersonal smell one always associated with hotels, stopping-off places. She had to wriggle Sarah out of her clothes like a two-year-old. (She'd had an accident some time or other without taking her clothes down: she bundled them away quickly so as not to embarrass her.) If it had been anyone else she couldn't have stood much more. Her head ached and she felt exhausted, unslept. It was like some dreadful dream, rushing out in the rain to go to her. She'd visualised all kinds of terrible things. And there'd been another little scene earlier on, before he left. The same thing all over again: wanting to know was the relationship sexual, and if so how. And now this. Incapable, incoherent. But she got all her clothes off at last, and her hair up, and turned her about and popped her into the bath. After a few minutes the girl was better. But sat awkwardly, with her arms across her breasts in that way young girls had. A natural modesty which was rather lovely, made her ache for her somehow. It was such a shame: and she wanted to protect her, to preserve what was left. She reached over and took her arms gently down and gave her a soaped flannel and said perhaps she'd like to get on with it now?

'No, don't go.' And got hold of her arm suddenly with both wet hands and pressed her lips to it. 'Stay with me: I have to think. Or must you go?' - looking up into her face. Her eyes were clearer now: she seemed more sensible of what she saw.

'Not if you don't want me to. Not right away.'

'Thank you.'

She put the pan cover down, and spread a towel over it, and sat there because everywhere else was heaped with clothes and things.

'What happened?' she asked as she sponged herself. 'With him I mean. Why did he make a scene?'

'Oh it was nothing much. He was jealous of course, but nothing much.' She watched the white bubbles lace across the girl's brown skin, then added: 'Just one of those things. He was bound to find out sooner or later.'

'I guess so.' She held the soap in her hand, looked at it a moment. 'But I wish later. I wish it hadn't happened right now.'

'Darling, we'll just have to learn to live with it.'

'Yes, I know. It doesn't bother me too much: it's you I was thinking about. If he was really jealous he could make things nasty for you.'

'I don't think so, darling. At the moment he's angry, naturally. But he wouldn't dream of bullying anyone: he's not that sort of person at all.'

'But then when he's not angry any more he'll be hurt and then maybe you'll begin to feel guilty. And then you won't want me around.'

'You're a hopeless little so-and-so. When you get out of that bath you're going straight to bed.'

'But I have that rehearsal. What time is it?'

She looked at her watch.

'It's only just gone two. You'll feel much better for a sleep. An hour at least.'

'You're not going to stay with me?'

'No. I want you to rest.'

'But I'll see you after the concert, like we arranged?'

'Yes, you will.'

She got out of the bath suddenly, broke from the water like a brown Venus, and semi veiled in the vapour that rose on the air.

'Have you finished?'

'Yes. I never stay long in the bath.' She switched a towel off the rail and threw it round her shoulders, dabbed at herself hurriedly. She seemed suddenly distracted and in a tearing hurry, as though something had got into her head that she didn't want to think about.

'I'll have a sleep, like you said.' And then looked desperately at her. 'You look so sad, so tired.'

'Darling, no. I didn't sleep well, that's all. But it will pass.' She got up, took the towel from her. 'Here, let me help. And what about this bad, wicked girl? Whatever does she look like?' Taking hold of her face, and turning it so she had to look at herself in the glass.

'Oh my God.'

'Yes, indeed. And unless she gets some sleep all her admirers are going to be very disappointed.'

'I will sleep, I promise. But you won't run away from me or anything? I'm scared soon as you go I won't ever see you again'.

'Sweetie, don't make it any more difficult. Please. Now

come along, kiss me instead.'

She reached up her arms and pressed her nakedness against her.

'I will. Yes, I will. Hey,' she said suddenly. 'I lost my ring. I remember: those kids took it from me.'

And something struck at her too when she saw the bare finger, the girl's frightened, deprived, bewildered expression. She felt the same quick leap of horror, remembered Anthony's words last night - that she'd no more come back to London than fly in the air.

'I've had it ever since - years, I've had it.'

'Well now,' she smiled, holding her tightly, 'your luck will change. Come along, darling, kiss me. And get a bathrobe on, or something. Goodness, look. You've made me all wet.'

SARAH

She woke suddenly, feeling desolate and helpless in a way she'd never done before. She couldn't have been asleep long: there was no change in the light. The same crepuscular gloom as when she'd got into bed. (Mrs Stankovich had drawn the curtains across before she left.) But it was like when you wake from a dream and you haven't woken at all really, but still dreaming, and everything is touched with horror.

She reached out and poked the clock round to have a look. Yeah, just under an hour. But zowee, not just an ordinary hangover: she couldn't think what. But like there was nothing, no ground under her feet. And, standing looking at her, the pop-eyed policeman doll in his shoddy little uniform. She reached out again and picked him up, stood him on the pillow. The glassy blue eyes wobbled and jumped and then were still. She looked at his pink baby face a minute, then put him down and turned on to her back.

The half light came across the ceiling in bars of varied quality, degrees of intensity. It was very quiet: she heard nothing, only the clock. She'd not really looked at the room, she realised, since she came. Just a suite of rooms. It didn't make sense now either, didn't say anything to her. Just another room. Nothing to catch on to, nothing familiar. And tonight she'd sleep here for the last time. She shut her eyes, turned her face away. All she wanted just now was to sleep and not to have to think about anything. But the doll pressed into her face and she caught hold of it again, meaning to put it back on the cabinet. Only now she was wide awake and her mind reeled suddenly like it had got some sort of shock, and then began to race. She sat up, looked around the room. She was thirsty and her head began to hammer in that way she knew it would, but she hardly noticed it. She threw the clothes aside and got out of bed, snatched up the bathrobe lying across it. First thing was to get them to send up a dictionary. It was stupid, but she wanted something concrete, something she could step off from. So she rang down and asked them, would they send up a dictionary? Then she straightened the bed and, time she'd done that, the bell hop was there with the book.

She just wanted to see what it said, and then she'd be all right. What did they call it? Oh yeah. That'd be under S. (Wasn't she a poet or something? She didn't know a lot about poetry.) Unnatural sexual relations between women

- she read it three or four times, then put the book down. Yeah. Well. (But Jesus, didn't those guys know anything about anything?) And that, she guessed, was the way he saw it too. Anthony Stankovich. He saw it as unnatural. She didn't mind for herself: it didn't bother her at all. But she wasn't married to anybody. She didn't have to see it dirtied and then thrown back at her. (Yeah? Who was she kidding? She didn't give a -). SO ALL RIGHT, she knew what she had to do. She had to make a phone call: she had to call Mrs Stankovich.

But first she'd straighten that curtain: it wasn't quite closed and let in an ugly shaft of light. Like that. Now it was palpable, the half light, and not quite real. It was like she was swathed in the dark, like the dark as soft as silk was all wrapped around her. (But this room with its flowers, its heavy curtains - how the hell did she ever get caught up in all this luxury?) So maybe this just wasn't happening and she really hadn't woken but was still dreaming.

When, at the other end, the phone began to buzz she suddenly wondered had she gone off her head or something? It seemed a horrible loud and real sound, right there in her ear. Bzz, bzz: nobody answered yet. She'd only to put the receiver down now –

Too late.

Who was it?, Mrs Stankovich asked at the other end. And then, tentatively: Sarah?

'Yes. But don't ask any questions, don't say anything more.' (She had to keep her voice low, it sounded so horribly loud here in the semi dark. And she didn't want, if Cassidi was hanging about outside, for him to hear or anything.) 'I'm not coming back to London. I don't want to see you again.'

There was a sort of stunned silence. She ought to have put the phone down only she was hanging on to it like for life and couldn't let go. And it was so stupid, so clumsy. It was like reading lines out of a book, like she was repeating after someone. Something she'd been told to say.

Darling, it -

'No, don't say anything. You'll be glad sometime.'

But no, Mrs Stankovich said, she didn't understand.

What did she mean? Was it a joke? For God's sake to say at once if it was a joke.

She felt sick inside, like she'd accidentally trod on a beetle or something. What was dreadful was Mrs Stankovich sounded so different, had never used the word 'God' before, and she could almost see the way she must be looking - frightened, angry. Angry in the way people got angry when they were desperate.

'I have to go now. Good-bye.'

She put the phone down and just stood there a minute looking at it.

Okay. So now they all had it the way they wanted. So now what? Drink? (There, on the table, was the two-thirds empty brandy bottle. You can MARtell the difference - something like that. In a magazine she'd seen somewhere. Yeah, on the flight over. Funny how it seemed just yesterday. But she pretended she hadn't seen the brandy: it was too real, that.) Pot? She'd never tried it, hadn't dared. She was scared stiff of drugs. All these kids shooting their mouths off about sex and drugs and that: it was pathetic. She knew only a few people who'd actually smoked pot, let alone anything else. Maybe this was exceptional, maybe not. She didn't go much to the places where they were supposed to do that sort of thing, so she didn't know. So not pot. The show, in any case, must go on. (This was classic: just like in a movie.) Always, the show must go on. (How corny could you get?) And so she'd go on singing jingle jangle songs *ad infinitum*.

She went back to the bed, picked up her watch and checked it off against the clock. Then wound it and put it down again. First she had to go wash her hair. And must take away the hair under her arms. She hated doing that but it wasn't correct if you didn't. Not with no sleeves. Didn't matter if she was a folksinger or what, she couldn't have hair under her arms. (Who objected then? Like you're a guitarist but nobody wants to know you got horny left-hand fingers, ladies shouldn't have.) Oh yeah, and there was another call she had to make.

'I want to call New York please.' (There was a wait before she could get through.) 'Joe? Sassy. You can fix those TV dates: I'll go talk to Cassidi about it now. What? No, I forgot - he wasn't here at the time. What? Yeah, I guessed he would be. Yeah, straight back. Why? Did you have some idea of me doing a home tour? No, tour. T.O.U.R. Yeah. Like the Universities you mean? Well, I don't know. I hadn't planned on doing anything right away. We could always talk about it.'

That's his girl. Oh, and good luck tonight. (In that stupid, cosy way he talked.)

'Yeah, thanks. I'll need it.'

Yeah, that was another bloody creep.

SARAH

There were faces on all sides, at the back of the platform too, and thousands of hands clapping. What Cassidi called a capacity house. The applause began as soon as she ducked the curtain - someone switched it back, held it high for her like in Oranges and Lemons. Which was a good thing because otherwise she'd have got herself all tied up in it, or something like that. She always did something stupid. Like now, going up the steps. One two three four five steps then trrrip!, and only just saved herself from falling. Bong! (The guitar.) Oooh, the people all gasped. (A lovely big smile, all white teeth, for the curtain guy who jumped forward to help, and all her lovely hair hanging down, and the damned dress that fitted her like a glove and was hot as hell, and she had to mince her steps so as to not to pull it apart.) Yeah, oooh. Her bloody leg. Then, carrying her instrument, awkwardly across the platform. The platform seemed bigger and emptier than it had seemed at the run-through even, like a big shallow island of light, and she always felt awkward going out on stage alone. Kind of gawky and knock-kneed. (The way she had to walk in this dress.) And diminished somehow. But not so small that she didn't feel as conspicuous as hell.

She waited a minute, smiling, then made her bow. And then all the lights went down and the spot hovered uncertainly before picking her up. (Mistake.) The auditorium seemed to fall back suddenly: way back, like a big open mouth all dark and spongey and no teeth inside. And she diminutive on its lip, looking in, while she got the strap over her head and shifted the capo up one fret. (It wasn't easy, standing: the instrument always gave some discomfort.) Then, smiling again, said what her first item was going to be and there was more applause and then a respectful silence. (English audiences were so polite: she didn't know if she liked it or not. It made her a bit uneasy.) She brought her elbow to bear, slipped the strap a little and the neck lifted. (The spot flashed on the machine head and for a minute it was like everywhere she looked there were small burning suns.) So on with the intro and then, as an accompaniment to her voice, Dm G Dm Gm Dm at a nice snappy pace and her fingers crossing the fretboard and back again like the legs of a pale spider. But a bit automatic. She had to work really hard to produce anything like a good sound, with both her voice and the instrument. And then her mind would wander off again. Nobody seemed bothered, so maybe it didn't notice like she thought it must.

Once over the opening verse, she took a look along the rows of seats in front. (It was the kids at the back of her she was sorry for, but she wasn't paid to turn her behind on the auditorium.) Here and there, a programme fluttered. Somebody's hand went up, moved quickly down again. All the girls had long hair, looked like herself. But the faces were vague, nebulous, merged with the background. Beyond the mike, with its perforated cylindrical head, it was all a desert. (Mrs Stankovich wasn't there of course, she hadn't expected her to be.) The mike was all she had, and this portion of platform picked up by the spot. The rest was just a mirage. Now and again someone moved, or coughed. But except for that, and the occasional small click or whistle when she negotiated a chord change, and the polite cataract of applause between items, it could have just as easily have been a dream.

She got through the first part of the programme without knowing really what she was doing, but they were bringing the place down when she came off stage. Then the curtain fell back behind her and she was alone in the lobby and suddenly it was quiet. It was so quiet she felt like she was trespassing. A light burned here in the passage, but kind of hallowed like before a shrine. The passage went off at an angle after a few steps. There were signs that said Emergency Exit, and arrows pointing, and a fire hose, and all dark teak wood and low overhead. And so quiet the silence hummed, and not a soul. Another passage, and then the door that said Conductor's Room. She went in, put on the lights.

She'd a sudden idea she'd find her here, waiting. Or that she'd come in a minute or two, knock at the door. (It couldn't happen of course: they didn't let anybody in backstage. Cassidi could see her if he wanted but she'd said not to bother her during the interval, please, she preferred to be on her own. Anybody else must wait at the Artist's Entrance. Or, by invitation, in the Green Room when the concert was over.) But nobody knocked and it was so quiet her skull felt like an eggshell - anyone could have put a spoon through it. It was like the room was vacuum sealed - the whole building had this sealed off atmosphere, like nothing ever got inside, not a speck of dust even. It was the sort of place you could live a nightmare in if you got lost. She wondered she didn't achieve a state of weightlessness like men in space. And nothing, no one. Only the low, dark, slatted wood ceiling, and the four walls, and the gentle glow of the wall lights, and the thick green-grey carpet, and the angular sofa opposite, upholstered in grey, and the looking-glass there on the left with its array of bulbs (but she hadn't put them on), and the telephone next the looking-glass, and the wardrobe shut away there on the right where she'd hung her coat when she first came in, and the two light wood chairs with their shiny black seats, and the small upright piano. It all looked back at her with such polite deference, such bland discretion, she could have shouted out loud. It wouldn't make any difference if she did: nobody would hear. You could die in here and nobody would know about it, and the room would remain aloof.

She stood her instrument against the piano, opened a door on the left and went into the lavatory. There was a handbasin too, and shower. And all shut off from the dressing-room: a room within a room. The lavatory had a curtain. (Quaint, because who could see you in here?) After, she washed her hands in the basin. But the sound of the water running in the basin seemed so loud she turned the tap off while she lathered her hands. They'd be leaving their seats she guessed, the audience. Or most of them. Going for a drink perhaps: she could have used one herself.

She closed the door after her, went to the glass and combed out her hair. Her reflection didn't mean anything, she hardly saw it. All she felt was how alone she was. (Except for the waiter guy who brought the pineapple juice she'd asked for earlier. She nearly hit the ceiling when he knocked at the door.) Here she was, in this room, alone. And somewhere along this empty passage and that, through the hive-like core of the building, up a flight of stairs or down, there were three thousand odd people all in love with her. She knew as little about them as they did about her, was almost as unfamiliar with what they saw of the building as they were with what she saw. And this - combing out a strand of hair and trying to get something of the same feeling from it - this was what they loved. This hair, this flesh, this shadowed armpit, these clothes. And it was nothing. Flesh hung on bones, and fabric on flesh, and it was nothing. It was now, only now as she stood here in this small room, that she knew what it was all about. (Or had she known all along?) She hadn't loved Mrs Stankovich at all, or only for selfish reasons. She'd hitched a ride, then thrown her over. It had got too hot for her, the whole thing. Yeah, those were the facts. No kidding herself she was some sort of heroine: she hadn't sacrificed anything much. All that with the dictionary was just an act, so her conscience wouldn't bother her too much. But worse than that, a whole lot worse. She didn't give a damn. She'd have done it all over again if somebody had asked her. She felt sorry, sick even, but nothing more. No real guilt. And it was this that scared her. She was like a zombie or something, a dead thing. But dead-alive. Jesus, yes: dead-alive.

She cried a little, just stood there with her hand over her face and cried. But the crying didn't help any: it was too late. They had her, all of them.

It yawned at her, as she went back along the passage where her footsteps didn't sound even, that there'd be a tomorrow and a day after that. But under the curtain she went and up the steps and the preliminary clatter of applause was the spoon through her eggshell skull. But, like she did now, she'd be smiling and bowing all over France. And in between times? Just driving on from one gig to another and sleeping in scabby provincial hotel rooms. If she could find some meaning in it, or anything at all, she'd be better. But like she was burned out, an empty shell, and there was nothing. Like she'd absorbed, become saturated with the rot of those she had to deal with. Yeah, they won all right.

'This next,' smiling as she picked at the strings, tightened one here and there, 'is unusual.'

Respectful silence.

'Because it's a happy song.'

Much laughter. She waited till they'd done, then bent her head and spoke like to herself only. Softly.

'It makes a change I guess. It's all about a girl who's going to see her sweetheart again after a long while. She loves him very much.' They laughed again at this, maybe because she made it sound like that wasn't possible. She hadn't meant to. 'But it doesn't say if she saw him or not.' The last gust of laughter blew away on the scented air (what was it they were blowing through the air conditioning?), and up came the guitar again and, making out she loved them all (maybe she did), laughing her face off at them, she shouted out the tune she knew so well it was like eating last week's bread. Or like she was miming for a TV show or something, and the disc going round and round and she just soundlessly opening and shutting her mouth. But she kept on singing because what else could she do? Nothing. Jesus Maria, nothing.

Mariana Villa-Gilbert
(1937-2023)

was born on 21 February 1937 in Croydon, South London. Villa-Gilbert studied art and sculpture, but her heart's ambition was to become a writer. Her first novel, *Mrs Galbraith's Air,* was published by Chatto & Windus in 1963. She published five other novels with the publisher over the next decade: *My Love All Dressed in White* (1964), *Mrs Cantello* (1966), *A Jingle Jangle Song* (1968), *The Others* (1970) and *Manuela: A Modern Myth* (1973). A short story collection, *The Sun in Hours*, the final published work in her lifetime, came in 1986. In the 1990s Villa-Gilbert moved to Cornwall and retreated from public view. She continued to write, however, and her literary papers - recently acquired by Special Collections at the University of Exeter - contain many unpublished manuscripts. Villa-Gilbert died in 2023. Lurid's new edition of *A Jingle Jangle Song* is the first republication of a Villa-Gilbert novel since the 1970s.